W9-DDK-110

033317 0278454

THIS BOOK IS DUE FOR RETURN
ON THE LATEST DATE SHOWN BELOW

6/00	81335	81257
038451	- 4 JUL 2001	093663
026201	2 6 JUL 2001	038737
81345		035084
033430	- 5 FEB 2002	81024
3/01	080988	075074
0 4 APR 2001	8200?	07211
1 7 APR 2001	81288	81024
1 8 JUN 2001	069201	8119?
	81036?	021490?
- 3 OCT 2001	076268	023040?
	81029	045748
	093518	024610?
	87	0294452
	018801	8
	0204446	038642
	018809	034666
	81029	020444
		021357?

CAMERON
IN THE GAP

Philip McCutchan

Chivers Press • Thorndike Press
Bath, England   Thorndike, Maine USA

This Large Print edition is published by Chivers Press, England, and by Thorndike Press, USA.

Published in 1999 in the U.K. by arrangement with Severn House Publishers Ltd.

Published in 1999 in the U.S. by arrangement with Chivers Press Ltd.

U.K. Hardcover ISBN 0–7540–3809–2 (Chivers Large Print)
U.K. Softcover ISBN 0–7540–3810–6 (Camden Large Print)
U.S. Softcover ISBN 0–7862–1964–5 (General Series Edition)

The text of this Large Print edition is unabridged.
Other aspects of the book may vary from the original edition.

Set in 16 pt. New Times Roman.

Printed in Great Britain on acid-free paper.

British Library Cataloguing in Publication Data available

Library of Congress Cataloging-in-Publication Data

McCutchan, Philip, 1920–
    Cameron in the gap / Philip McCutchan.
    p. (large print) cm.
    ISBN 0–7862–1964–5 (lg. print : sc : alk. paper)
    1. Cameron, Donald (Fictitious character)—Fiction. 2. World
War, 1939–1945—Fiction. 3. Large type books. I. Title.
[PR6063.A167C29   1999]
823'.914—dc21   99–14885

CHAPTER ONE

The new orders had come when HM destroyer *Burnside* had completed fuelling from the Admiralty oiler off Kyle of Lochalsh in western Scotland; having rounded Cape Wrath on passage from the fleet anchorage at Scapa Flow, she had expected to steam westwards into the North Atlantic to make a rendezvous with the homeward-bound HX convoy out of Halifax, Nova Scotia. She was about to cast off from the oiler when a motor-cutter was seen coming off from the shore, her bows throwing up a spray that caught the moonlight in a thousand glitters.

The Captain, Lieutenant-Commander Fanshawe, lifted his binoculars and studied the motor-cutter. 'Seems to want to come alongside, Cameron. There's an officer in the sternsheets. Chosen a damn good moment, I must say! Belay unberthing till we see what's in the wind.'

'Aye, aye, sir.' Cameron, Officer of the Watch, passed the order fore and aft as the motor-cutter came alongside the quarterdeck and the officer scrambled out from the sternsheets. Cameron watched him coming for'ard along the starboard side of the upper deck, making for the bridge.

'Well?' Fanshawe barked ill-temperedly as

the officer saluted. 'Who are you?'

'From NOIC, sir.' The officer, an RNVR sub-lieutenant, reached into the inside breast pocket of his bridge coat and brought out a sealed envelope which he handed to the Captain.

Fanshawe ripped it open and took it across to the chart table in the rear of the bridge. Thrusting his head through the canvas screen, he switched on the light. Cameron, listening to the subdued hum of dynamos from the destroyer and the oiler and to the soft lap of water against the plates of the ships, suspected a change of orders. He was not wrong. Fanshawe stepped back from the chart table, giving nothing away yet.

'Thank you,' he said curtly to the officer from NOIC's staff. 'Take your boat away as soon as you can.'

'Aye, aye, sir.' Once again the officer saluted, turned about and clattered down the ladder. As soon as the motor-cutter had cast off, Fanshawe passed the orders to take the *Burnside* clear of the oiler. When the destroyer was heading out through the Inner Sound he called down to the fo'c'sle. 'Number One!'

A duffel-coated figure looked up. 'Sir?'

'Come to the bridge as soon as you've secured for sea.'

'Aye, aye, sir.'

Behind Fanshawe, Cameron grinned to himself. That was just like Father. Number

2

One would as a matter of routine have come up to report that he had secured for sea, but Fanshawe liked to dot all his i's and cross all his t's. He was precisc to the brink of mania, an old woman in seafaring garb. When Henry Williamson, First Lieutenant, reported to the bridge, all Fanshawe said was, 'We have fresh orders, Number One. Negative the HX escort. We rendezvous at 0900 hours with *Burgoyne* and *Brahmin* from Scapa and a convoy from the Clyde. The rendezvous will be ten miles north-west of the Mull of Kintyre. The three of us will provide additional escort.'

Williamson asked, 'What's the convoy, sir?'

Fanshawe looked pained, the moonlight etching deeper the heavy lines of his face. 'There's a degree of secrecy, Number One. A degree of secrecy.'

*   *   *

Burnside slid fast through calm water, oily-smooth water with the island of Raasay to port. Making the turn past the Sound of Raasay towards the headland of Rubha Hunish to enter the Little Minch, Fanshawe increased revolutions until the destroyer was steaming at thirty-four knots, not so far off her maximum speed. There were some two hundred and fifty miles to go for the rendezvous. Cameron watched the great hills of Skye slide away as the ship turned to his

3

helm orders towards Harris and then made south for the Skerryvore Light to the south-west of Tiree. All was peace; yet Cameron knew it was no more than a surface and very temporary respite. The war which, like the Great War, was to have been over by its first Christmas, had dragged on into 1942 and was still in a nasty phase of heavy ship losses, both escorts and merchantmen. It had turned largely—mostly—into a convoy war so far as the Navy was concerned. Cameron had had his share of that and more; so had Fanshawe. Bitter experience had taught Fanshawe that the worst always happened when the Captain left the bridge; thus he hardly ever left it. He was there now, hunched on his seat at the fore screen, head turning this way and that. Pilotage waters—it was natural for the Captain to be there, but Cameron knew the area well enough for Fanshawe to have taken advantage of peaceful conditions to get some much-needed sleep. He'd had virtually none during the whole ten days of their last escort.

A little before Cameron was relieved from his watch at 0400 the starboard bridge lookout reported, 'Ship astern, sir. Two ships I reckon, sir, closing.'

Cameron and Fanshawe swung round, bringing up their binoculars. By this time daylight was not far off; the dark shapes, still hull down, were easily seen. '*Burgoyne* and *Brahmin*,' Fanshawe said. That was all; he turned his back as signals were exchanged, resuming his watch ahead, hunched like a zombie. A few minutes later Cameron handed over the bridge to Mackenzie, the RNR sub-lieutenant, and went below to his cabin to snatch some sleep. When three hours later he went to the wardroom for an early breakfast there was only one other officer present: Mr Bartram, Gunner RN. Bartram looked up.

'Morning, Mr Cameron. Know where we're off to, do you? What's the buzz from the bridge, eh?'

Cameron grinned. 'Father doesn't originate buzzes, Guns, you should know that by now.'

'Yes, reckon I do an' all,' Bartram said grumpily. 'One thing I'll take a bet on—it's not a bloody boiler-clean in Londonderry, more's the pity!' He munched toast liberally covered with marmalade. 'Could do with some leave, I could. I'm too old for this lark, watch on stop on.' He paused, then said, 'A little bird tells me we're going south. Got your whites with you, eh?'

Cameron nodded, but asked, 'Why south?'

'Because,' the gunner answered heavily, 'seeing as we're not going west after all, there's no other perishing way we *can* go.'

'Could be north, couldn't it? Murmansk?'

The gunner shuddered. 'No! They can't do that to me! Wouldn't be Murmansk, anyway. We'd be rendezvousing farther north, somewhere off Loch Ewe. Back where we

5

come from ... they wouldn't be sending us down this way.'

*   *   *

They met the convoy and its escort dead on the time set for the rendezvous. Cameron, supervising the part-of-ship work on the quarterdeck with his divisional petty officer, PO Pollen, watched with a stomach-sinking sensation as the ships closed. There were two large troop transports, one ex-Orient Line, the other ex-P & O. There were six cargo vessels of tonnages ranging from eight to twelve thousand tons; three tankers; three ammunition ships, bulky and vulnerable with their thin unprotected sides and the single antiquated 6-inch guns mounted aft and manned by gunners of the Royal Artillery. Not an especially large convoy numerically, but clearly important, for with them was a massively strong escort: the battleships *Nelson* and *Rodney*, the aircraft-carriers *Victorious, Indomitable, Eagle* and *Furious*, the cruisers *Nigeria, Kenya, Argyll, Auckland, Cairo, Sirius, Phoebe* and *Charybdis* with no less than twenty destroyers and four corvettes, the destroyer escort being under the overall command of no less than a rear-admiral.

From behind Cameron a voice said, 'Bloody hell!'

Cameron turned. It was the gunner.

6

Bartram went on, 'It's not meant for taking auntie to the seaside for a paddle, Mr Cameron, we can be sure of that if nothing else.'

'What does it all suggest to you, Guns?'

Bartram looked at him quizzically. 'The same as it ought to you, I reckon. Eh?'

'Malta?'

'That's right. Maybe not all for Malta—some of 'em may go on to the Middle East. But Malta can do with a bit of relief one way and another. Last I heard, they was eating rats and half the island bombed to buggery.' The gunner slapped the shield of the after 4.7-inch twin mounting. 'These little wonders are going to be busy once we're east of Gib. Before, like as not.'

Cameron nodded. A troop and ammunition convoy would never be allowed to pass in peace—and come to that, the mixture was an uneasy one. Fast troopships were better off steaming independently than shoved in with stores and ammunition carriers . . . *Burnside* was now taking up her station as signalled by the Senior Officer of the escort: arse-end Charlie, as Bartram said sardonically, right in rear to shepherd stragglers and protect the convoy from attack astern. The destroyer was heeling over sharply under full helm, cutting a wide swathe through the deep blue water of a fine day. Above them the sky was almost a Mediterranean blue, with a few thin, elongated

7

white clouds moving before a light wind. Some ten miles to the south-east lay the great bluff of the Mull of Kintyre and beyond it the waters of the Firth of Clyde. On the bridge the Captain, once in his station, steadied the ship on a westerly course to stand clear of the Northern Irish coast above Rathlin Island. The convoy would remain on this course for some while before turning south, making out into the North Atlantic to put as much distance as possible between itself and the German aircraft and U-boats from Brest and the other ports in occupied France. Fanshawe, as usual exercising extreme caution, gave little away to his ship's company. As the forenoon watch proceeded towards the welcome pipe Stand Easy he used the tannoy to broadcast to all hands. But all he said, in his clipped voice, was, 'The ship is under orders for Gibraltar.'

'Spot on, I was,' Bartram remarked to his gunner's mate, PO Garter. 'It's bloody Malta for sure.'

'Up the Gut again, eh?'

Bartram gave a laugh, a rueful one. 'Not me, Tommy. Too bloody old for that lark. All right for some. Last time I was up the Gut was when I was in the *Resolution* back in thirty-six.' The reference was to a certain thoroughfare in Valletta, more properly called Strada Stretta but known to generations of British naval ratings as the Gut. Up the Gut was a synonym for wild women and strong drink, the place that kept the Navy's medical branch in business. Bartram added, 'Even if we make the Grand Harbour in one piece, Tommy, chances are we'll not be getting much shore leave. They'll have us back at sea before we've bloody had a chance to refuel.'

Garter agreed, scratching a formidable chin. There were all too few escorts in this war. It was all sea-time now, no more swinging round a buoy or alongside the dockyard wall like in the piping days of peace. It was a different Navy, too: nearly all reservists who didn't look at things in quite the same way as the peacetime RN. They were all right, Garter reflected, once they'd learned port from starboard and not to march off on the wrong foot. All right, but not what he'd been used to. Some of them, the hostilities-only ordinary seamen, were what he called hoity-toity, unsure of their standing and thus inclined to be either too deferential to the petty officers or inclined to look down their high-class noses ... pre-war, many of them had been young men on the first rungs of professional ladders, teachers, solicitors, people of that sort, and a gunner's mate didn't rate intellectually however important he might be to their lives afloat in an alien environment. Garter, however, wasn't really worried: what he didn't know about guns hadn't been invented yet, and the most important thing about the old *Burnside* was her guns. You lived or died by

9

them. It didn't matter a sod if you were a lawyer or a dustman, just so long as you knew how to fire the guns.

Below in his minute sick bay, the doctor, Surgeon Lieutenant Michael Fleming, also heard the Captain's broadcast and reflected that if the ship's company were given leave in Gibraltar he would thereafter be busy attending upon the inevitable results and never mind the useful articles handed out liberally on request by his Leading Sick Berth Attendant. They didn't always work; they could split in action. Fleming gave an involuntary sigh as he checked round his medical stores. There were boxes and boxes of the bloody things, more of them than there was of ether or morphine or bandages . . . the British sailor was somewhat one-track-minded when ashore. Fleming, who had qualified three years earlier and had been all set to sit for his MRCP when war broke out and projected him into the RNVR, felt that his talents were being wasted, that he was nothing more than a panderer to the Contagious Diseases Act. Of course, it would be different when action came. To date, he hadn't been in action; he'd had shore appointments mostly and since he'd joined *Burnside*, only a couple of months earlier, the ship had been lucky, experiencing no hits, no casualties in her attacks on U-boats or while dodging the bombs dropped from the far-ranging German aircraft, and seeing no

10

surface action at all. Fleming had removed an appendix and that had broken the monotony and helped to justify his presence aboard. He had amputated a finger caught by the breech block of one of the 4.7 guns, a lesson to the OD concerned to use nothing but a clenched fist in future to ram home the projectile; and he had cured a number of boils. It wasn't much. But he had a feeling this trip was going to be different; he didn't know why. Perhaps it was the presence of the battleships and so many aircraft-carriers. The Admiralty didn't chuck that sort of weight around for no purpose.

Fleming laid a hand on the shoulder of LSBA Trott. He said, 'I want everything ready, just in case.'

Trott looked offended. 'Already is, sir. *Always* is.'

'I know, I'm not criticizing, Trott. But just have another check round, will you?'

'If you say so, sir.'

'And list any deficiencies. We should be able to make good in Gibraltar.'

Trott pushed out his lower lip. Doc was, in his way, as much of a fusser as the skipper. Perhaps all officers were, when at sea. *Burnside* was Trott's first ship; before that it had been RN Barracks, Devonport. But Trott was reasonably certain that the only stocks that would need replenishment after Gibraltar would be the French letters. He grinned to himself; the last doctor had gone on fourteen days' leave with a box of twelve dozen and had come back looking like the wrath of God.

*   *   *

The convoy took its final departure from the Bloody Foreland off the coast of Donegal. As Ireland faded astern the Captain called a conference of officers in his sea-cabin. It was a tight fit but they all crammed in. Fanshawe spoke in a low voice, as though Hitler was lurking in the forced-draught system. Confirming what Mr Bartram had said earlier, he indicated that the convoy was proceeding through the Mediterranean. Some of the merchant ships and some of the escort would carry on to Alexandria. The rest, including *Burnside*, *Burgoyne* and *Brahmin*, would detach to the relief of the Malta garrison, taking in desperately needed troop reinforcements plus food, weapons and ammunition.

'The garrison's hanging on by a thread,' he said. 'It's absolutely vital we get through, and get through intact. Any losses will have a very serious effect on Malta's ability to survive. I stress that—*any* losses.' He cleared his throat, his gaze flitting over the faces of his officers. 'What is perhaps the most vital ship of all will rendezvous from the Plate as we close the Gibraltar Strait. That ship is the *British Racer*. She's carrying a full cargo of aviation spirit.

12

Malta's air defence must be kept operational.'

He happened to be looking at Cameron. Cameron's mind went back to the start of the war: in September 1939 Malta's entire air defence had lain in three old Stringbag aircraft, Swordfish biplanes nicknamed Faith, Hope and Charity. It had been a miracle that Malta had survived; it must never return to such terrible defencelessness. Malta was not only a valuable base but also a symbol that had sustained the British Fleet since the days of Nelson. For Malta to fall was unthinkable: it would rank with the sinking of the *Hood* the year before. Britain needed good news, not bad. Fanshawe was going on, his curt tones passing the orders for what was clearly expected to be a hard-fought convoy. He started with Darcy, an RNVR lieutenant a few months junior to Cameron.

'Darcy, as my Gunnery Control Officer, you'll be exercising action as frequently as possible before Gibraltar. It will not appear in Daily Orders, I shall order it at short notice. Mr Bartram, you and your gunner's mate will drill the guns' crews to the maximum state of efficiency and you'll see to it that the torpedo-gunner's mate does the same with the tubes.'

'Aye, aye, sir.'

'Any armament stores required will be available at Gibraltar. Mr Canton, the same applies to oil fuel.'

Canton, the Commissioned Engineer,

nodded.

'If any defects develop, I'll signal my requirements ahead to the dockyard. You will keep me fully and instantly informed.'

'Yes, sir.'

Fanshawe turned to the RNR sub-lieutenant. 'Pilot, make certain you acquire all the latest Notices to Mariners and put in your chart corrections to the Mediterranean folio. With special reference to the deep minefield between Tunisia and Sicily. Now, are there any questions?' Fanshawe paused, expectantly, head lifted. 'No? I must say I'm glad to know of your self-confidence,' he said with a touch of sourness. Be very sure that I shall bring any inadequacies to your attention most promptly. Yes, Harcourt, you have a question?'

Harcourt, the RN midshipman, seemed suddenly self-conscious, wishing he hadn't raised his hand. He said, 'It's only a personal matter, sir. Not a question. The Master of the—'

'The Master of the *British Racer*. Yes. I was coming to that. Captain Hamilton Harcourt—I noted the name in the list of convoy. Your father?'

'Yes, sir.'

'Don't allow the fact to interfere with your duty to the safety of the convoy as a whole,' Fanshawe said. He was about to dismiss the officers when the sound-powered telephone whined at him from the sea-cabin bulkhead.

He took it up. 'Captain here. What is it?'

Cameron, who was standing close to the telephone, heard the words. 'Bridge, sir. Admiral reports a German heavy cruiser ahead, spotted by reconnaissance aircraft from *Eagle.*'

'I see. Has the Admiral passed any orders?'

'Not yet, sir.'

'Sound action stations,' Fanshawe said. He replaced the receiver. 'Well, gentlemen, we have the enemy ahead. This is the start. It's going to be a long business.'

As he left the sea-cabin the action alarm was sounding throughout the ship.

CHAPTER TWO

The cruiser had been identified as the *Solingen*, heavily armoured along her sides, carrying eight 8-inch guns and bristling with HA armament. Already she was under attack by the aircraft from the carriers, who had turned into wind to fly off their squadrons of torpedo-bombers; and she was now reported as having turned away to run for it. As Fanshawe remarked, the German had been unlucky. Presumably out of radar range, she wouldn't have picked up the convoy's presence until the reconnaissance planes had revealed the fact of a carrier in the vicinity, something

15

that would have indicated the strength of the escort. She might have caused havoc with a lightly-guarded, normal convoy, the sort she would welcome for attack. With this one, she hadn't a chance.

'One thing seems reasonably certain,' the Captain said. 'The security's been good. So far, that is.'

Behind Fanshawe's back, Cameron nodded. No leaks; had the German been warned from Brest of the exceptionally heavy escort he would have kept well out of the vicinity until reinforcements became available. No one risked valuable cruisers on a forlorn hope. The signal lamps were busy now, passing orders from the Flag: the battleships were to remain with the convoy, as were the destroyers and corvettes. The cruiser force was ordered ahead at full speed to engage and destroy. Cameron watched as the lean, camouflage-painted cruisers detached, their white wakes streaming away behind them. Balls of smoke could be seen distantly over the horizon ahead as the enemy ack-ack sent up shrapnel to burst around the aircraft of the Fleet Air Arm. Soon the British attacking force was hull down; minutes later they had vanished, but as the convoy proceeded the sounds of battle could be heard. Soon after this a signal came, general from the Flag, passing on the action reports from the spotters in the battleship's fighting top: *Cruisers are engaging and enemy has been slowed*. It was not long after this that a vast explosion was heard, shatteringly, and a pall of thick black smoke rose over the horizon. It didn't have to be the German; but there was no more gunfire and when the British cruisers came back to rejoin the convoy they were seen to be all present. A storm of cheering came from the merchant ships and the escort.

'One less to worry about,' Fanshawe said, 'but it's not all beer and skittles—is it, Cameron?'

'You mean the German'll have reported by wireless, sir?'

'Yes, I mean exactly that. He may not have known our full strength, but from now on we've lost our advantage.'

*　　*　　*

'Poor sods,' Leading Seaman York said, without sounding particularly sorry. The convoy had come up to the spot where the *Solingen* had gone down. There was nothing left beyond the usual debris, smashed and charred woodwork, broken boats, life rafts, seamen's caps and other personal gear, all floating on an oil-covered sea licked with flame. That, and bodies, heads down in the water or on their backs with sightless eyes lifted to heaven. The cruisers had picked up survivors but there hadn't been many. It was

17

not an unusual sight of war at sea but although Leading Seaman York had seen it all before it made him, this time, for no reason that he could think of, ponder on the fact that at any moment something similar could happen to the *Burnside*. He could become like those bodies, a floating derelict that would bloat its way around for a while till it burst. It was a matter of luck, that was all—and the degree of alertness of the blokes up there on the bridge. Not just their alertness: a lot depended on their ability to assess situations, and to a large extent on their particular mental outlook on life and death. In short, whether or not they were death-or-glory boys, wanting to show they were Nelson come back to life. The skipper, York fancied, was a death-or-glory boy in his quiet way. Nothing flamboyant, but dogged. The sort that never gave up.

York sighed and, as PO Bunney, petty officer of the fo'c'sle division, came for'ard he started to look busy. Bunney expected that of his senior leading hand; Bunney was young for his rate and thought that noise and bullshit was efficiency, daft git. York could lose him when it came to seamanship, and they both knew it, which made Bunney worse. Leading Seaman York had survived many a Bunney in his time in the Andrew. Salt horses like this one who believed, like the mariners of old, that every hair on their bodies was a marline-spike and every drop of blood a drop of good

18

Stockholm tar. Or gunner's mates who were so stiff with bull and boot-polish that they didn't move, they jerked. Crushers, as the regulating petty officers of the provost branch were called on account of their big feet, acted like a load of pint-sized Lord Chief Justices. Screw the lot, York thought as he began a bit of chivvying. He didn't chivvy enough and PO Bunney raised his voice in complaint, picking his nose at the same time.

'Get 'em shifting, York. Work to be done, you know, it's not a bloody make-and-mend.' Bunney knew he was right under the eye of the skipper on the bridge. Long in the leg, he stepped over the starboard anchor cable and pointed. 'What's that, eh?'

'Panter,' York said.

Bunney pulled up short, staring, thin nose twitching. 'Eh? You trying to be funny?'

'No, PO. It's Ordinary Seaman Panter.'

'Yes.' Breath hissed through Bunney's teeth. 'I know that, thank you very much. I wasn't pointing at him. I was pointing at the load of crap down by the fairlead. What is it?'

York said briefly, 'Dead shite-'awk.'

'Tell Panter to get rid of it.'

York raised his voice. 'Panter. Repel dead seagull.'

Bunney's face flushed and he seemed about to utter when the Captain leaned over the bridge screen. 'Petty Officer Bunney,' he called.

19

Bunney saluted rapidly and snapped to attention. 'Yessir!'

'That seagull. How did it happen?'

Bunney opened his mouth then shut it again. He looked at Leading Seaman York. York answered for him. 'Kind of crash-landed, sir. That, and old age I reckon. Probably 'ad an 'eart-attack, sir.'

There was a half smile on Fanshawe's face. He said, 'Yes, very likely. It's unusual for a seagull to come to grief like that.'

'Yes, sir.'

Fanshawe waved dismissingly and York went back to the job in hand, which was washing down the fo'c'sle. He was shaking his head in wonder about the skipper. Fancy worrying his nut about a perishing shite-hawk in the middle of a world war. Maybe he was looking on it as an omen, as though it had been an albatross. He hadn't shown signs of superstition before, not to York's knowledge. It made York think about it more deeply; it was dead right shite-hawks didn't normally do that, but no doubt they had to die sometime. Pity they had to choose the old *Burnside*, right at the start of a convoy like this one, all big guns and portentousness.

*   *   *

The drills and exercises proceeded. Petty Officer Garter was in his element as he chased the guns' crews for their lives and back again. In the director, the GCO, Lieutenant Darcy, noted times and reported to the Captain. Little by little the timing improved—the timing from Exercise Action to All Guns Ready—shaving off the vital seconds that could make all the difference to the outcome of battle. Fanshawe was pleased, though he didn't show it. A Captain, in his view, should never appear satisfied. There was always a higher state of efficiency to be achieved and no one must be allowed to become complacent. Fanshawe's father, a retired vice-admiral now serving as a commodore of convoys, had impressed certain things upon him when he had passed out from the Royal Naval College, Dartmouth; one of these was that a ship's company should be more scared of the Captain than they were of the enemy. That way, there was no holding back in action. Fanshawe, however, knew himself to be incapable of instilling that particular feeling in any man. He hadn't the forceful personality that it took. But he had seen the point and had set himself to find another way, and his way was to remain withdrawn, imposing himself as a kind of enigma who might jump this way and might jump that—and also never to appear satisfied. He found that kept his ship's company on its toes and it was less fatiguing than trying to scare. In any case there were three well-established scarifying factors in existence to back any commanding officer, these powerfully thought-provoking factors being known as King's Regulations and Admiralty Instructions; the Articles of War; and the Naval Discipline Act. Captains of HM ships never stood naked and alone.

Yet another report came down from the director. A record had been achieved and Darcy's voice was expectant.

'Thank you, Darcy,' Fanshawe said into the telephone, taking it over personally from the communication number on the bridge. 'We'll do it again. Cameron?'

'Yes, sir?'

'Fall out the guns' crews.'

'Aye, aye, sir.' Cameron bent to the voice-pipe and passed the order down. When everyone had fallen out, Fanshawe piped Exercise Action and the whole thing was gone through again. Noise was everywhere. Shouts from the captains of the guns, shouts of *commence, commence, commence*, the metallic noises from the breech blocks as the dummy projectiles went home. It was all a good thing, of course; practise made perfect—in theory anyway. But sometimes seamen could be driven too far and then they became bored and bolshie. It wasn't as though most of them hadn't had plenty of real battle experience; Cameron would have preferred to see them given some respite while it was still possible. Once they were into the Med, they'd get no

22

sleep at all until they brought the convoy safely into the Grand Harbour at Malta.

Two days out from the Mull of Kintyre, the orders came from the Flag for the alteration south. Cumbersomely the merchant ships swung to port, keeping their stations as best they could with the difference in the pitch of their screws and with their widely differing engine-room capacities. The escorts came round with them, *Rodney* and *Nelson* and the aircraft-carriers swinging in stately fashion like mountains graciously preparing to receive Mahomet. The more manoeuvrable cruisers and destroyers and corvettes seemed in comparison to run like sheepdogs.

When the turn was complete and the whole convoy steadied on a course a little east of south Fanshawe said, 'Cameron, send down to the First Lieutenant. I'd like a word.'

Cameron passed the message. Within two minutes Williamson was on the bridge.

'You wanted me, sir?'

'Ah, Number One.' Fanshawe turned from a binocular sweep of the seas ahead. 'Yes. I want to exercise sending away the seaboat. You never know.'

'True enough, sir.' The First Lieutenant was surprised nevertheless.

'You sound doubtful.'

'It'll need permission from the Flag, sir.'

'Yes, I know. I'm sure the Admiral will approve any attempt to achieve full efficiency,

23

Number One. Yeoman?'

The yeoman of signals approached. 'Yessir?'

'Make to the Flag: Request permission to exercise my seaboat's crew.'

'Aye, aye, sir.' The yeoman got behind his signalling projector and made the Flag's pennants. The acknowledgement came back and, after a pause, the answer. The yeoman approached the Captain again. 'Reply, sir. Permission granted but boat is not repeat not to be slipped, sir.'

'Thank you.' A spot of colour had appeared in Fanshawe's cheeks and he said drily, 'As if I would. Carry on, Number One. When you get word from me, lower to just above the waterline. I want you to time the whole manoeuvre precisely from the moment I pipe the seaboat's crew and lowerers of the watch. I have in mind a time I wish to achieve, and I shall repeat the exercise until I have achieved it.' He pulled a stop-watch from his pocket. 'I shall check you, Number One. Now, Cameron, the pipe.'

Cameron bent once again to the voice-pipe. The boatswain's call sounded round the ship: For Exercise, Away Seaboat's Crew and Lowerers of the Starboard Watch. Fanshawe pressed a button and started the timing.

*　　　*　　　*

Leading Seaman York was the coxswain of the

seaboat for the starboard watch. In charge of the lowerers was Leading Seaman Dewhurst. York was a three-badge man; Dewhurst's left arm bore no badges beyond the fouled anchor that signified his rating as a leading hand. That anchor was by way of being a courtesy, or anyway a consolation prize. Dewhurst was a failed CW rating. Recommended for a commission, hc had gone to HMS *King Alfred* for officer training but had failed to pass out as a sub-lieutenant RNVR. His papers had been marked RTU and back he had gone to the barracks at Pompey to await draft. As was customary in such cases, he had been rated leading seaman but few of his messmates were willing to accept him as such. News travelled fast in the *Andrew* and Dewhurst's history was well known aboard *Burnside*. It was only rumour that put his failure down to lack of power of command and a general scruffiness in his appearance, but rumour happened to be spot on and the wonder was that he had ever been given a recommend in the first place. York, for one, regarded him with total contempt. In York's opinion it was an insult to all leading hands to give a killick to a failure as a kind of sop. There was no soft option about being a leading hand; you needed personality to sustain leadership over a bunch of your mates when you lived, slept and ate with them twenty-four hours a day.

York wasn't surprised when Dewhurst was

the last man to obey the pipe; his only surprise was that Jimmy the One didn't give him a proper bollocking, but Jimmy was too easy to be a real First Lieutenant and never mind that he was dyed-in-the-wool RN from Dartmouth. It was York himself who gave the bollocking, sotto voce.

'Bloody little drip, letting the bloody watch down.'

Dewhurst flushed—bridled was the word if York had thought of it. 'Mind your own business.'

'It is my business, *Mister* Dewhurst. Me an' my lads, we'll be in your bloody shaky care, right, when you lowers us. If you drop us in the drink, I'll 'ave your balls, that's if you've got any.'

Dewhurst turned his back. York was a big boor and the only thing to do was to disregard him. York saw his boat's crew in, then embarked himself. He fixed Dewhurst with a meaningful glare, holding fast to a lifeline, trusting his life to the steel-wire stay overhead. The Captain called from the bridge, Williamson gave the word and Dewhurst passed the orders for lowering. 'Start the falls ... lower away together ... gently does it—'

York growled, '*Handsomely*, silly tit.'

'No interference from the boat,' the First Lieutenant said.

Dewhurst turned to him; then turned back as he heard a shout from York. The for'ard fall

26

was running out faster than the after one. Dewhurst began to panic, said, 'Oh, Christ,' and gave the wrong order. The for'ard fall went out even faster and the seaboat's bows took a downward slant, tipping the crew, who were saved from a slide only by their grip of the lifelines. The lowerers were making an attempt to belay the falls when Dewhurst, his face crimson, moved for one of the ordinary seamen at the for'ard fall and gave him a shake, a vicious one. The youth fell back against another of the lowerers and the fall ran away again, too late now for the First Lieutenant to rectify the situation. The bows of the seaboat, still unslipped, took the surface and, with way still on the ship, the boat began to fill as it scooped up the water, swaying out to starboard on the end of the fall and beginning to overturn. Most of the crew kept their grip on the lifelines but two men failed to do so. As they went overboard and began to drift astern they were seen from the bridge. Fanshawe reacted fast, stopping engines and ordering the wheel hard over to bring his ship round towards the two men.

As he did so there was a sudden change in the note of the Asdic. The operator reported, 'Contact, sir—'

Fanshawe swung round. 'What was that?'

'Contact, sir, bearing red nine-oh, drawing aft. I believe it's a submarine, sir.'

CHAPTER THREE

'Attacking,' Fanshawe said briefly. 'Yeoman, inform the Admiral and Captain(D).'

'Aye, aye, sir.'

'Port fifteen, maximum revolutions, stand by depth charges. Sound action stations.'

Cameron passed the orders down to the wheelhouse. The note of the Asdic remained high, the pings almost continuous. There was a rush of men to their stations as the alarm rattlers sounded, rasping and urgent. The coxswain, Chief Petty Officer Dickens, doubled to the wheelhouse and took over the helm as Fanshawe ordered more port wheel. Dickens reported, 'Cox'n on the wheel, sir!'

'Right,' came Fanshawe's voice. 'Wheel amidships.'

'Midships, sir. Wheel's amidships, sir.'

'Steady.'

'Steady, sir. Course, two-six-five, sir.' *Burnside* rushed on under full power. Watching the gyro repeater in front of the wheel Dickens said, 'Those poor sods in the drink. Bloody rotten luck.' By this time the First Lieutenant had got control of the seaboat's falls; the boat had been hoisted clear of the water. There was no response from the wheelhouse staff to Dickens' comment but the faces were glum enough. What a way to go, if that was what was

28

to happen to the two men who'd gone over. All because some wet killick couldn't take charge. But they should be all right; after all, they'd had their cork life-jackets on, like anyone else in a seaboat's crew, and this wasn't winter nor was it the Denmark Strait or some where along the terrible run to Murmansk or Archangel. As Dickens thought about the abandoned men he heard the orders being passed on the bridge, not for him but for the guns.

'All guns stand by ... target left. Fire when your sights come on, Darcy.' Then the Captain spoke directly down the voice-pipe. 'Cox'n?'

'Sir?'

'Target surfacing. I intend to attack by gunfire.'

Dickens, holding the wheel steady with one hand, scratched reflectively at the stubble on his cheek. Surfacing, eh! For what? To be destroyed by the 4.7-inch armament, or to surrender? Maybe she'd been damaged in some earlier attack and didn't fancy any more depth charging. Thirty seconds later there was a violent concussion as the main armament opened. The wheelhouse seemed to expand and contract again; cork insulation, shaken loose behind the paintwork, spattered the deck. Then the Captain's voice, high, frantic.

'*Cease firing! All guns cease firing!*'

There was a curious stillness as the guns fell silent. The coxswain felt his flesh creep and he

29

got there before the word came down from the bridge: it wasn't a U-boat, it was a British submarine. Talk about a cock-up all round. Then Cameron's voice came down the pipe, confirming the submarine's identity. He said, 'Thank God we only straddled her, Cox'n. No damage or casualties.'

Dickens felt a rush of anger. He said, 'She didn't ought to have been there, stupid bastard, not without showing up on the plot. What about our lads in the drink, sir?'

'About to be picked up,' Cameron answered. The Captain had already informed the Admiral of his intentions. 'Starboard fifteen.'

Dickens swung the wheel over. Later, there would be an enquiry, bound to be. That submarine CO deserved to be court martialled, hanging around right smack in the path of a bloody great convoy like this one. Some blokes needed their heads read. Dickens simmered down: there could be a reason. You shouldn't judge without the facts.

*   *   *

The seaboat, got away at last, returned alongside for hoisting on the falls with only one of the men retrieved alive; the other, although his life-jacket was intact, was dead. His head was a mess, the skull fractured; he had hit it hard on something when he went over. Stripey Pond . . . a good seaman, a three-badge AB, sea-daddy to most of the young ordinary seamen, a tower of strength and a fount of seamanship knowledge. Pollen, quartermaster PO, had known him twice before, once in the old *Hawkins* on the China station, once up the straits in the *Royal Oak*, the time in Malta when there had been all the hoo-ha about Bandmaster Percy Buzzard who'd thought the Rear-Admiral commanding the battle squadron had called him a bastard, and had made a complaint that had shaken the whole Med Fleet from truck to keelson. Able Seaman Pond had been one of the witnesses. As a seaman Pond could have lost any present-day PO or leading hand, but he'd never wanted promotion, just a quiet life. Never mind the difference in their rating, Pollen and Pond had been friends. When Pollen got the buzz about Leading Seaman Dewhurst's part in the lousy rotten business he took Dewhurst aside and gave him a piece of his mind.

'Little stinker. As a leading 'and you're no more bloody use than a wet day in Manchester. You killed Stripey Pond far as I'm concerned.'

'I'm not responsible for any man's personal clumsiness, PO.'

Pollen almost struck him; but discipline held. He said, 'You're not even responsible for yourself by the sound of it. Thought you'd like to be an officer! Thank God the Admiralty had more sense. Just you keep out of my way from now on, that's all. Else *I* won't be responsible either.'

Pollen turned away. Dewhurst, ashen-faced, went back to his cruising station at Number Three gun aft on the quarter-deck. He wondered why he wasn't already in the rattle; he had seen the First Lieutenant making for the bridge and guessed he was the subject of a report to the Captain. Maybe to the Admiral, when the skipper had to account for the loss of a man. Dewhurst, avoiding the eyes of his gun's crew—there was a nasty silence in his vicinity—stared out aft at the tumbling white wake that streamed back to the north. That wake seemed to tumble in tune with his mind. It wasn't fair; he hadn't had a fair crack of the whip. He should never have been ploughed at *King Alfred*; he was good officer material, had the education and the wider vision of an officer even if he hadn't the technical ability of a leading seaman. As an officer, you dealt with men differently, you were apart from them in a much more positive sense. You just couldn't live on intimate and level terms with men and at the same time give orders. Dewhurst's face puckered: God, it was so bloody unfair! For a start, there had been his father. It had been desperately hard to explain to a major-general on the staff of Southern Command that his son had been sent back to the lower deck.

On the bridge Fanshawe also was cursing the way things had happened. On the face of it, from his First Lieutenant's report, there was little doubt that Dewhurst should be punished by disrating down to AB. On the other hand, Leading Seaman York had shot his mouth off at an unfortunate moment, and Fanshawe was extremely reluctant to have York put in his report as indirectly contributing to the tragedy. York was the best leading seaman in the ship and Fanshawe wanted to see him as a petty officer. A black mark would be no help at all. Fanshawe was naturally aware of York's record: there had been a previous black mark. York had already been a PO and had lost his rate because he'd brought a half-bottle of whisky back aboard a battle-cruiser, the *Renown*. He had now worked off his time for rehabilitation and could put in a request to be rated up again. But not if he was in the report.

'I'll think about it, Number One,' he said.

Williamson hesitated. 'It's fairly urgent, sir.'

'Yes, I take your point. No one'll have any confidence in Dewhurst—I see that only too well.'

'He can't be allowed to hold his rate. That's my view. What's going to happen in action, sir?' Williamson's rather stolid face was troubled. 'It's too much of a risk.'

Fanshawe blew out his breath and lifted his binoculars to stare round the horizon. Lowering them again he said, 'I'll let you know, Number One. If there's to be a charge, how would you propose wording it?'

'Failing to take charge as a leading seaman and causing the loss of a man overboard.'

'Somewhat serious in that case.'

'Very serious, sir.'

'Not just disrating. Detention Quarters ashore.'

'The ship would be better off without him, sir.'

Fanshawe nodded. 'I'll bear that in mind, Number One.' It was a possible solution; in a few days' time they would enter Gibraltar. There might be a way of landing Dewhurst, but it would need careful thought. Fanshawe turned away from Williamson, who took the hint and, lifting a despairing eyebrow at Cameron, went down the bridge ladder to the upper deck. The Old Man was too cautious by half and too much caution could be as dangerous as too little. Both Williamson and Fanshawe happened to have lived in Southsea for many years before the war, both fathers being RN and living the typical life of penurious naval officers in rented furnished flats in the dockyard town; and Fanshawe's mother had been well-known in naval circles for her often-repeated dictum: 'It needs well thinking about.' Fanshawe had been carefully nurtured on that particular aphorism.

*　　　*　　　*

'Roll on my bloody twelve,' Leading Seaman

York said in the messdeck, drinking hot cocoa before going back on watch.

'You've been in more than twelve years already, killick,' Ordinary Seaman Franks said.

'You shut your face. As an OD, you speak when spoken to, what you wasn't.' York took a long swig at his mug. 'I was soliloquizing if you want to know, because I'm bloody chokker with this lot.'

'You'd never settle down ashore, you know you wouldn't.'

'No. That's another reason I'm chokker. Bugger being in, bugger being out—and one o' these days I'll 'ave to go ashore. That's if I live long enough, o' course,' York added judicially, not wishing to provoke providence. He gloomed for a few more moments, finished his cocoa, then started singing untunefully in a deep bass. 'Roll on the *Nelson*, the *Rodney*, *Renown* . . . this two-funnel bastard is getting me down . . .'

'For Christ's sake shut up, damn you!' a voice, high and breaking, screamed at him from the other side of the messdeck. York stopped, mouth open, eyes belligerent. Ponderously he heaved his full stomach clear of the mess table and got to his feet. He moved across the corticene-covered deck almost like a panther and stood facing Dewhurst, who was peering down from a slung hammock and holding the coarse blanket up to his chin. Like a woman in her bloody boudoir, York thought,

35

awaiting rape and not liking it.

'Just kindly repeat that, *Mister* Dewhurst,' York said in a polite tone, grinning like a devil.

'Leave me alone.'

'Sulking, are you, and I don't wonder at it, to be perfectly frank and honest, *Mister* Dewhurst. Case of 'ighly-strung nerves too, judging by the squeaky voice. Not to bloody make mention o' the immense danger inherent in talking to me like you did. Wonder you bloody 'ad the guts.'

'Will you go away and leave me alone?'

'Well now, *Mister* Dewhurst, I reckon the answer to that is no.' Leading Seaman York reached out a hand and laid it on the blanket, which he jerked away with a sudden hard wrench. Then he put both fists beneath the body of the hammock and heaved upwards. Like a sack of potatoes, Dewhurst fell out and landed on the deck, partially saving himself by a wild grab at the hammock lashing. Reaching out again, York prised the hand loose, seized Dewhurst by his vest, which he wrapped in a knot around his fist, and propelled him backwards across the messdeck, cheered on by the off-watch seamen.

'Now,' York said. 'You've asked for it. You're going to get filled in. Put your bloody 'ands up and watch out.' After the warning York moved fast. He had just aimed a fist towards Dewhurst's jaw when a sharp voice came from the doorway into the galley flat.

'Hold it, York. Now what's all this?' Mr Bartram moved in, square and solid. 'What's the trouble, eh? Or have I guessed?'

York nodded. 'I reckon you 'ave, sir, yes.'

'Leave him alone. That's an order. There's war enough going on outside. You bloody mad, York?'

'That's about right,' York said grimly.

'Hold on to it then, if you value your hook. Leading Seaman Dewhurst, get back into your hammock if that's where you've come from.'

'Yes, sir.' Dewhurst moved away.

'Leading Seaman my arse,' York said in a loud voice.

The gunner took no notice of that. He said quietly, 'Now, I didn't see any of this. Nor did anyone else, all right? But what I didn't see isn't to happen again or I may just get my vision back. Understood, York?'

'Yes, sir.'

'Just remember, then.' Bartram paused. 'It looks like this isn't a good moment for what I came about, but I'll go ahead now I'm here. The Captain's given permission for Pond's effects to be auctioned in the First Dog tomorrow, weather and Hitler permitting also, that is. Proceeds to Pond's wife and kids. Auction'll be held here in his mess. Up to you, York, to make the bids as high as you can, right? You all know the drill. I'll start it off with a donation.' He handed a pound note to Leading Seaman York. York almost whistled; a

37

pound was a fair lot out of a warrant officer's pay of around three quid a week. York would back that with plenty of encouragement to the lads to bid to the limit. The gunner left the messdeck after a sweeping glance around, a glance that took in Dewhurst back beneath his blanket with his rump turned towards the mess. Bartram was thinking: poor sod. You couldn't help feeling a degree of sympathy. His position was an unusual one, unique to this war with its temporary RNVR commissions. To be half-way to being an officer and then go back to the lower deck was enough to put anyone's mind in a twist, for a while anyway.

*　　　*　　　*

The convoy came round Carnero Point to enter Gibraltar Bay at 1800 hours four days later. Prior to this the rendezvous had been made with the *British Racer*, a fast twin-screw ship built not long before the outbreak of war with government backing as a vessel fit to act when required as a naval auxiliary. The tanker, with her load of almost six million gallons of aviation spirit, had taken up her station in the centre of the convoy after the exchange of signals, which included one from the tanker's master to Midshipman Harcourt in the *Burnside*. This was reported to Fanshawe by the yeoman of signals.

'Inform Mr Harcourt,' Fanshawe said. The

message was a simple one of pleasure in sailing in company with a son; but Fanshawe's mind went ahead to things far removed from pleasure. A father could watch a son drown, or the other way round, and nothing to be done about it on either side. For himself Fanshawe much preferred to be half the world away from his own father when both were at sea, and not only for the reason of sinkings: fathers, at any rate when in the same service, could be restrictive.

Midshipman Harcourt was on the bridge as *Burnside* reduced speed to enter the inner harbour and go alongside in the destroyer pens while the convoy anchored off in the bay. Fanshawe saw him looking towards the *British Racer*. He said, 'Leave will depend on what I'm told by the Tower.'

'Yes, sir.'

Just a moment later the signal came from the Chief of Staff to Rear-Admiral, Gibraltar, made by semaphore from the Tower in the dockyard, general to all ships of the convoy and its escort: *Commanding Officers and Masters will attend upon the Rear-Admiral at 2000 hours. Shore leave may be given until midnight.*

'Acknowledge,' Fanshawe said briefly to the yeoman. He took his ship in through the breakwater and headed her up for the pens. When the lines were ashore and made fast, he turned to Harcourt. 'You can have the motor-boat, snotty,' he said. Then he went below for an hour's urgently needed sleep before cleaning into fresh whites for the Rear-Admiral's benefit. His sleep was disturbed by nightmares centring around Leading Seaman Dewhurst. After the conference ashore he mentioned the matter to the Chief of Staff, a four-ring captain RN. He got no joy; acidly, the Chief of Staff said this was no time for drafts and replacements. Fanshawe must make the best of what he'd got and it was up to him to cope with his domestic problems. Leading seamen unfit to hold their rate should be disrated and not wished on to someone else, and this sounded like a clear case for disrating.

When Fanshawe returned aboard his face was grave. Saluted over the brow by Williamson, he said, 'Come to my cabin, Number One. I'd like a word with Dewhurst's divisional officer, too—Cameron, isn't it? Unless he's gone ashore.'

'He's aboard, sir.' The First Lieutenant sent the gangway messenger to find Cameron, who was in his cabin catching up on the never-ending paperwork to do with divisional matters: entitlements to good conduct badges, kit muster forms, time put in for higher rates, requests to be considered for courses leading to higher non-substantive rates in gunnery, torpedoes, Asdics . . . personal problems such as arose when husbands had been long separated from wives. Reports, assessments, a

40

mass of detail. Cameron had long ago learned that a conscientious officer's day was never done, that when you took time off you always left something unfinished. Life was more placid on the lower deck, where off watch was off watch. He went along to the Captain's cabin, knocked and entered. Fanshawe, rubbing at weary eyes, said, 'Ah, Cameron. As I've just told the First Lieutenant, the convoy's under orders to leave Gibraltar at 0100. I just hope we don't get too many drunks among the libertymen, that's all! Too many bloody bars in Main Street. However, it's Dewhurst I want to see you about.'

'Yes, sir?'

'My report's gone in, of course. About the man lost. There was obvious carelessness and some action'll have to be taken. That's obvious too. I've no doubt in my mind that Dewhurst should be disrated, but I don't want to see York suffering because of him.' Fanshawe gave a self-deprecatory grin. 'I've said all this before. I'll admit I'm in a quandary. I'd like to disregard the whole damn thing. But since a man died, I can't. Can you see a way out, Cameron?'

'Are you asking me as Dewhurst's divisional officer, sir?'

'Yes.'

Cameron frowned. 'I think it would have a pretty devastating effect on him, sir. Mentally, he's close to the brink—'

41

'I know. But the doctor isn't prepared to recommend he be put ashore on medical grounds. He doesn't agree there's a case or anything like it. In the meantime I have my ship to think about.'

Cameron said, 'Yes, sir. I'm afraid I haven't any way out to offer. Except that . . .'

'Yes?'

'I think I'd give him another chance. What happened has rocked him, I know that. He may pull his finger out now.'

'Have you spoken to him?'

'Yes, sir. Off the record, of course, just a friendly chat. He's going through hell. Being chucked out of *King Alfred* was pretty recent, and now there's this.'

Fanshawe nodded. He said, 'I can understand his feelings. I'm going to procrastinate, Number One,' he added to the First Lieutenant.

Williamson was as stolid as ever; he was an officer of little imagination but he knew King's Regulations backwards. He said, 'But there'll *have* to be a charge, sir. That can't possibly be avoided. It's not just that a man died.'

Fanshawe narrowed his eyes. 'Go on, say it, Number One. The ship's company will smell favouritism because Dewhurst's father's a major-general.'

'In my opinion, yes, sir.'

Fanshawe's voice hardened and he raised clenched fists to his forehead. He said, 'Jesus

Christ, as though this bloody war isn't enough. We're about to sail smack into what could turn out to be the bloodiest convoy that ever tried to get through the Med. The Rear-Admiral didn't mince his words, I can tell you. On top of that we have a possible accusation of arse-crawling to the brass. Bugger the brass—it's certainly not that!'

'*I* never thought it was,' the First Lieutenant said. 'It's just—'

'All right, all right.' Fanshawe calmed down. 'Number One, you know the book. Get together with the cox'n and work out something for now that doesn't *have* to carry severe punishment. Simple inattentiveness or something—you know what I mean. Put him in my report and I'll remand him for further consideration. If as Cameron says he pulls his finger out, then I can just give him a reprimand later on and we'll have him drafted back to barracks on return to the UK. He won't be able to do an awful lot of damage there.'

*   *   *

As Officer of the Day Cameron was at the brow when the main body of returning libertymen was seen coming back from the delights of the town, as near to midnight as possible: the last drop of beer had to be crammed in since it might be a long while

43

before they saw any more. Gibraltar in wartime was an oasis of bars and prostitutes under the bright lights of apparent peacetime, an illusion really, but an alluring one. Men from the fleet customarily made the most of it, the more so when they were bound east through the Med. Tonight they lurched back through the dockyard, singing. As they came aboard they walked with stiffly sober ostentation but they ponged like a brewery and some of them had to be propped up by their messmates. Cameron walked over to the other side of the quarterdeck. What he wasn't seen to have seen, he didn't have to take action over. In any case the ship couldn't steam to war stations with three-quarters of her company in the rattle. As the last of the libertymen lurched and belched their way for'ard, banging off bulkheads and cursing furiously, the destroyer's motor-boat came alongside from the anchorage and Midshipman Harcourt came aboard and saluted.

'Well, Mid. Find your father all right?'

'Yes, sir. When he got back from the conference.'

'What sort of run-up did he have from the Plate?'

'No trouble at all,' Harcourt said. 'Fair weather and no U-boats. Or surface raiders. But he's not looking forward to the Med. He looked pretty worried when he came back aboard.'

'I don't suppose he told you why?'

'No, sir. He's been like a clam ever since the war started.'

Cameron nodded and said, 'I can tell you it's not going to be a picnic, Mid. The Captain'll give us the full gen once we're away.'

Fanshawe did. Sharp on 0100 the ropes and wires were cast off while out in the bay the convoy shortened-in ready for the executive order to weigh. The destroyers and cruisers with the battleships and aircraft-carriers steamed into their stations and the great concourse of warships and their charges moved out beneath a bright moon to make the turn to port and steam below Europa Point eastwards into the war-torn waters of the Mediterranean. Once clear of the Rock, Fanshawe flicked on the tannoy.

'This is the Captain speaking. The ship will go to dawn action stations at 0400 and is likely to remain closed up until we reach Malta. With the dawn, action may come at any time. An attack by shore-based aircraft will probably be the first thing. After that, the Italian battlefleet is known to be in position off the westward approaches to the Narrows between Sicily and the Tunisian coast. They call it the Gap, out here. There's a deep minefield ... and it gives us little room for manoeuvre once we're in. While we're in the Narrows, strong air attack from Italian-based German dive-bombers is expected.' Fanshawe paused. 'It's vital that the part of the convoy detailed for Malta should get through. The Germans and Italians know this as well as we do. Intelligence received in London indicates that Hitler personally has ordered the convoy's total destruction. If we fail to get through, Malta is likely to fall. That is all, except that I wish you all good luck.'

Cameron noticed that Fanshawe's hands were shaking as he replaced the tannoy's microphone. Continual command at sea in wartime was heavy on the nerves.

*   *   *

Below in the engine-room Mr Canton, Commissioned Engineer, watched his dials and gauges, watched his engine-room artificers moving about quietly, eagle-eyed, watched the nozzles of oil-cans probing, then shifted into the boiler-room where the Stoker Petty Officer of the Watch, wiping his hands on a bunch of cotton-waste, was equally watchful but had half his mind on a woman named Maud, handy for a man when in barracks. Maud was married and so was the Stoker PO, but not to each other; Maud's favours were offered extra-maritally. Maud lived in Devonport—or had. When the mail had come aboard in Gibraltar there had been bad news. Maud's husband's

46

work—he was in a reserved occupation—had taken him to Okehampton. He and Maud were now living in a village close by; the village where the Stoker PO and his wife lived. Stoker PO Wantage sucked at his teeth, angrily. Talk about bloody awful luck; you could never keep things quiet in a village and in any case when he went home on leave his old woman would have a loving eye on his every move. Natural in a way when you only had a week or two together, but hard on a man who had a bit of crumpet down the road. He would have to watch himself, and in future Devonport itself would be a profitless place to serve in, not that he was likely to see much of Devonport till he got a draft chit from the *Burnside*, of course. Best be philosophical about it; he'd had a good run for his money over times past.

He turned as Mr Canton approached.

Canton asked, 'Everything all right, eh?'

'Fair enough, sir. Time we 'ad a boiler-clean if you ask me.'

'Chief Stoker's theme song is that. All you're after is leave.'

'Aren't we all?'

Canton chuckled. 'Course we are. They can stuff this war. All I can say is, I'd sooner be here than taking the bombings back home. Families . . . they're the ones who suffer. Night after night in the shelters, sod all to eat half the time what with the rations, hardly any fags and beer always off after about eight in the evening—what a perishing life, eh! Get any mail in Gib, did you, Wantage?'

'Yes, I did.' The tone was sour; not the note of really bad news received, but the note of unwelcome problems. Mr Canton knew PO Wantage fairly well and could make a guess that somewhere along the line a woman was involved. A woman in the family way, maybe. It was a funny thing about sailors; nearly all their problems were female, even in his own case but with a difference: Mr Canton was a pillar of the Elim Tabernacle. His problem was his wife, who was more of a pillar than he was in point of fact. When Mr Canton was at home with the old battleaxe he lost his status as Chief Engineer Officer and he didn't like it. It worried him that he didn't like his wife either; it was ungodly and one day he would suffer for it, but he couldn't help it. He moved on, back to the starting platform in the engine-room, eyes critical. In his own kingdom, Mr Canton was as pernickety as Fanshawe on the bridge. Stoker PO Wantage watched him go and then turned his thoughts back to his home problems. He was thinking nostalgically of Maud stepping out of her knickers when two things happened very close together: the alarm rattlers sounded and a heavy explosion came from the starboard side, seeming very close to the wafer-thin bulkhead of the boiler-room. Wantage was knocked off his feet and went sliding on his backside towards the furnaces,

48

all thoughts of Maud vanishing as he heard the sharp clatter of the HA armament pumping out shells.

CHAPTER FOUR

'GOD!' Fanshawe had his hands clamped tightly over his ears. The screaming was dreadful, shattering, rising and falling like the wailing of a banshee as the bridge became sticky with pumped-out blood. The yeoman of signals had a piece of metal through his right thigh, another through his right shoulder—big pieces, part of the bridge itself—and there were other injuries. The Surgeon Lieutenant was there, doing what he could—an injection of morphine which didn't seem to Fanshawe's overstretched nerves to be achieving much. Fanshawe set his teeth. Why didn't the man die? The screams were a kind of reproach, a terrible protest about the sheer futility of war. The death of a yeoman of signals wasn't going to be a lot of help to Hitler or Mussolini.

The screams stopped. They stopped suddenly, they didn't just die away as they might from the morphine's effect. Fanshawe, as his guns continued flinging shrapnel towards the attacking aircraft, forced himself to look down at the deck of the bridge. He met the doctor's eye; Fleming was looking as

49

though he might be sick at any moment, though he ought to be used to death coming in nasty guises. Fanshawe snapped, 'Can't you do something?'

'I've done all I could,' Fleming said. 'I just turned him over and everything fell out. The stomach . . . it was torn to shreds.'

The night was a warm one but Fanshawe felt deathly cold. He turned away, sick at heart as he saw further signs of carnage along his decks. The star-lit sky seemed full of bursting shells; it was like some gigantic firework display, but still the enemy aircraft were coming in. No one had expected attack from the air quite so soon after leaving Gibraltar, which had hitherto been outside the range of land-based aircraft. The noise was deafening, a continual roar of sound as the escorts fought back. Fanshawe called the engine-room, from where the Chief had reported sprung plates from a near miss.

Canton answered himself, sounding phlegmatic. 'Engine-room.'

'Bridge. How's it going, Chief?'

'There's a bit of water, sir, but we'll cope. The damage control parties are doing fine.'

'Keep me informed. If you want extra hands, you shall have them.' Fanshawe shut the voice-pipe cover with a snap. He ducked as a torpedo-bomber roared close above the bridge and as he straightened again he saw the trail running just below the surface, clear beneath the clustered brilliance of the stars. He shouted, 'Wheel hard-a-starboard!'

Cameron passed the order; the destroyer heeled sharply and the sea's surface rose up her port side. The Captain's order had come just in time; the torpedo passed astern, uncomfortably close, but a miss was a miss, for them at any rate. Passing on, the torpedo took one of the little corvettes right amidships and she blew up. There was a momentary impression of bodies flung into the air like grotesque puppets in the surge of flame and then there was nothing but burning wreckage.

Fanshawe said, 'Port ten. I'll look for survivors. Inform the First Lieutenant. Rig scrambling nets.'

When they went in, there was no one left alive. A few bodies floated, held up by their inflatable life-jackets. Turning away, Cameron glanced at his wrist-watch: they'd been in action just five minutes but it had seemed an age—an age before the great fleet carriers had flown off their fighter squadrons to weave in and out of the attacking aircraft. Once they were in the air, the British fortunes changed. A number of the enemy were brought down in the sea and others succumbed to the ack-ack fire from the escorts. As suddenly as they had come in, the enemy broke off and disappeared ahead towards Sicily. Cameron knew the pilots would be watching their fuel gauges closely.

With the dawn not so far off now, *Burnside*

remained closed up at action stations. When the sky lightened Fanshawe and Cameron, joined now by the First Lieutenant, scanned the convoy closely through binoculars. All the merchant ships were there still, steaming serenely on between the warships. So far, so good. But the escort hadn't been so lucky. In addition to the corvette two destroyers had blown up and one of the cruisers, the *Auckland*, was still fighting fires that had broken out fore and aft. Aboard the *Burnside* the only fatal casualty had been the yeoman of signals but a number of men had suffered badly from flying metal. In the boiler-room Stoker PO Wantage had received burns and bruises and was currently being attended to in the sick bay and wishing that Maud and not the LSBA was his nurse. The damaged engine-room plating had been caulked and shored up and should last into Malta if nothing worse happened. There would be a seepage and that was all.

Congratulatory signals were made from the Flag and Fanshawe passed them over the tannoy. 'This is the Captain. The Admiral has signalled his appreciation. The signal reads: *Well done every man. Keep it up and we shall win through.*' The tannoy clicked off.

Leading Seaman York was on deck, taking it easy in the lee of Number Two gun. He looked towards the flagship, steaming steadily and magnificently with its massive 16-inch turrets trained to the fore-and-aft line just like peacetime. York blew out his cheeks and made a rude noise. It was all very well for His Nibs the perishing Admiral. The battleship navy was a very different kettle of fish from the destroyer navy. In the battleships and battle-cruisers they lived soft, with spacious messdecks for the hands, a bloody great wardroom for the officers filled with armchairs and bottles of booze, stewards with napkins over their arms, all very pusser. Lovely cabins, especially the Admiral who even had a drawing-room all done out in chintz ... you needn't know you were at sea if you didn't want to.

'Now then, York. What's all this?'

York looked up and met the sardonic eye of Petty Officer Garter, gunner's mate. Never mind the night action, Garter was shaved and properly dressed in the rig of the day, Number Thirteens, whites with blue badges. There was a fresh smell of soap and toothpaste. Gunner's mates, Gunnery Instructors as they were usually addressed, they were as bad as admirals, full of bull. 'What is it this time, eh, GI?' York asked.

'On your feet and look. If you'd looked before instead of loafing, you'd have seen it. See?'

York got up and looked towards where the gunner's mate was pointing. There was a small fragment of cotton-waste adhering to the breech block of the starboard gun of the mounting, just visible if you had a magnifying glass. York made a great show of peering this way and that and seeing nothing. The gunner's mate stabbed with a finger, close to the offending fragment. 'Gun's bloody invisible beneath the shit. Get rid of it.'

Garter stalked away to find more faults. York sighed but felt fairly philosophical. Gunner's mates were gunner's mates and had to be put up with. You couldn't blame them. If you didn't have a loud voice and didn't use it when you had it, you never got made up to chief gunner's mate. And all said and done, they were preferable to that drip Dewhurst.

*　　　*　　　*

Midshipman Harcourt, acting as officer of the quarters on the HA guns aft, stood on the starboard side of the gun deck above the splinter screen, back straight, hands behind his back, looking ahead towards the *British Racer*. She was a trim, smart ship, one of the big tankers, all of 21,000 tons displacement, and in her and other ships of the British Tanker Company's fleet his father had spent much of his peacetime life sailing to and from the port of Abadan in the Persian Gulf, one of the world's hottest hell-holes. Tankers had always been tricky; oil fuel and refined spirit needed careful handling and there was a real risk each and every time the tanks were cleaned and even when loading and discharging. Smoking had to be very carefully regulated at all times; and any spark off metal could mean disaster. Now it was war and the risks were so immense as to be appalling if you thought too much about them. Harcourt knew his father didn't dwell on the dangers; but he himself did. There was a *rapport* between father and son that was not lessened by Captain Hamilton Harcourt's frequent chaffing remarks about the RN and its peacetime propensity to remain in harbour until the tin cans mounted to the accommodation-ladders. All very fine gentlemen were the RN officers but they made a type and not a breed. A naval officer in plain clothes could never be mistaken for anything other than what he was; Merchant Service officers came in all shapes and sizes but shared the one thing in common: they had certificates, not easily obtained, to prove that they were seamen. If they made a cock of anything thereafter, they were out on their ears. Certificates could be lost for incompetence, while in the RN, if you put a ship aground, you lost a little seniority and then went back to bugger up another ship. That was what Captain Harcourt said and Midshipman Harcourt knew there was a grain of truth in it. He himself had opted for the RN for a variety of reasons but was honest enough to admit to himself that chief among them was the fact that he didn't want always to be at sea. There was a life elsewhere and the odd shore appointment, in barracks, or doing courses, or on some shore-based admiral's staff, or acting as liaison officer with one of the RNVR divisions, would be very acceptable in the years that lay ahead of a midshipman.

His father had been always at sea except for his leave periods. His mother had reacted against that; Midshipman Harcourt was assumed not to know, but he did. He hoped his father didn't. For himself, if and when he married, he would want to spend more time with his wife. But he'd still wanted to go to sea as a career and the glamour of the uniform, the blue and gold, had had something to do with that.

Harcourt turned as Lieutenant Cameron came aft from the bridge. Harcourt admired Cameron; not many RNVR officers wore the ribbon of the DSC on their jackets. Cameron could have been RN if he'd wanted to. Rumour said he'd had a tough war already and had come out on top, starting on the lower deck as an OD. Harcourt, though his cadet days at Dartmouth had been tough enough, couldn't even begin to imagine what it must be like to live for months on end in a crowded messdeck and be chased and chivvied by all hands from AB up.

'Morning, Mid.'

'Good morning, sir.'

'Everything all right?'

'Yes, sir.'

Cameron looked at him closely and gave him a smile. 'Don't worry about your father. The whole escort's here to see he gets through.'

'That's just it,' Harcourt said. 'His ship's the prize, isn't it?'

'A moving ship's not an easy target, Mid, you know that.'

'They still go down.' Harcourt looked again towards the tanker, moving as solidly as the battleships and within her workaday limitations as smart. He said, 'My father told me once about one of the company's ships. She'd been loading refined spirit at Abadan and she was some way out into the Shatt al Arab. There'd been a small leakage from one of the tanks, so small that it hadn't been noticed, leading back to the loading berth. Someone at the berth chucked a fag-end into the water. The spirit caught and a spark flashed right the way along and blew the tanker sky high.'

There was nothing Cameron could find to say to that.

*   *   *

The next attack came in an hour after full light. This time it was the Stukas. From now on, there would be no respite for anyone and they all knew it. They had to grit their teeth and keep their sights fixed on Malta: each turn of the screws brought them closer, that was the only way to look at it, every minute meant progress. A scratch breakfast was being brought to the men at action stations when the enemy aircraft were reported from the flagship's radar. Breakfast was to have been unappetizing enough: tins of what the fleet knew as herrings-in—herrings in tomato sauce. That, and steaming cups of cocoa, a mixture to churn any stomach. Now even that would have to become a dream. Such men as had been stood down from the guns and depth charges and torpedo-tubes to bring the food or visit the heads now closed up at the rush. The moment the aircraft roared in, the ships were ready for them. An immense barrage went up.

Cameron had never seen anything quite like it; he had never steamed in company with so vast an escort before. It was an amazing scene. The merchant ships moved on sedately beneath the puffs of smoke, the bursting shrapnel. The sea was blue, as flat as a millpond, disturbed only by the streaming white wakes and the tumble of water from the bows as the cruisers and destroyers of the escort zig-zagged at high speed, manoeuvring to avoid the bombs and at the same time protect the vital convoy. Signals came from the Flag and from the Commodore of the convoy, the latter aboard the ex-Orient liner carrying troops. Another of the corvettes was quickly hit, taken on her bridge by a dive-bomber that hurtled out of the sky, seeming to come straight out of the rising sun to attack like a gigantic bird of prey. The bomb delivered, the Stuka zoomed up, almost standing on its tail. From *Burnside*'s fo'c'sle Leading Seaman York shook a fist towards the Stuka.

'Filthy bastard!' he yelled, his face showing purple between the white material of his anti-flash gear. Then he gave a wild cheer: from amidships the multiple pom-poms, chattering like a devil's orchestra, had scored a hit, or anyway York's opinion was that it had been *Burnside*'s ack-ack that had done it. The Stuka burst into a ball of flame that licked through the heavy black smoke, and plunged down into the sea.

On the bridge Fanshawe's view was the same as York's. 'One to us,' he said. He used the tannoy. 'Well done, the pom-poms!' He doubted if in fact anyone heard a thing through the racket. The din was making it difficult to pass orders, but the ship's company was trained to a high pitch and knew what was wanted of them. In the director, Lieutenant Darcy was keeping the guns on target as each presented itself. Or was, until the end came. And that, for Darcy and his director's crew, was when a shot-up Stuka came down and landed smack on top of them. Flame and smoke streamed.

Cameron yelled down the voice-pipe. 'Fire parties at the double!'

Chief PO Dickens told off the boatswain's mate to pipe the order but already the First Lieutenant was mustering the hands. The heat was intense as the hoses were run out; the fire took some while to bring under control. Pieces of shattered metal rained down on the bridge, some still red-hot. Fanshawe and Cameron found their uniforms burning, and beat at each other to put out the smoulder. Steam and smoke obscured the view from the bridge. It was Cameron who first saw the loom of a ship's side right ahead, and without orders from the Captain yelled for the wheel to be put hard over and the engines full astern.

Fanshawe wiped his streaming face as they came clear. 'Well done,' he said. 'That was close.' He looked like a scarecrow: his face and anti-flash gear were blackened, his white uniform was ripped in many places. Blood streamed down from his left shoulder but was disregarded. Below the director the Surgeon Lieutenant was ready with morphine but had to wait till the fire was out, knowing that it was already too late. After the fire had been dealt with, the axes got busy and the wreckage of the Stuka was pushed over the side. The Surgeon Lieutenant was proved right: there was nothing human left. The flesh had melted. Fleming shook like a leaf. What had been Darcy and the director's crew was now just scorched bones and a congealing pool of fat that had dripped down the shattered metal tracery. This was a very different way to practise medicine.

Mr Bartram, his face grey, made a quick inspection of the director when the metal had cooled and then reported to the bridge.

'Captain, sir. Director's kaput.'

'As I expected, Guns. Any hope of a running repair?'

'Waste of time, sir. Dockyard job.'

'Let me have full details. I'll report requirements to Vice-Admiral Malta on arrival.'

Bartram's mouth hung open. It took a strait-jacket mind to worry about the bullshit side at a time like this. Report my backside, Bartram thought, that's bloody routine, for now we haven't a director and that's what matters. He said, 'We'll have to go to quarters firing, sir.'

'Yes. Take a walk round, Guns. Have a word with the quarters officers. All HA weapons to keep firing till they get the word.'

'Aye, aye, sir.' The gunner turned away down the ladder. He knew what the skipper meant: a little bit of stiffening from an experienced old bugger. One of the quarters officers was the midshipman, still wet behind the ears; the others were RNVR one-stripers, not long out of *King Alfred* in Brighton. They hadn't experienced quarters firing before other than for exercise and might be rattled by

61

not having the comfort of precise orders passed to them. In quarters firing you had largely to make your own decisions. Mr Bartram went aft first for a word with young Harcourt, sweating like a pig and with one of his shoulder-straps bearing the thin gold stripe of a warrant officer dangling from its tapes, the button torn away by a piece of shrapnel that could have taken his head off but hadn't, luckily for Mrs Bartram back home. She was always dead scared he would never come back, more scared than he was. Bartram knew it was worse for those who spent their lives expecting a telegram from the Admiralty, much worse than for those, like him, out there fighting.

Bartram sweated up to the after HA mounting.

'All right, Mid? Quarters firing from now. You all set up for it, are you?'

Harcourt nodded. 'Yes, Guns. Any special orders from the bridge?'

'Just keep firing, that's all, blow the sods out of the sky. Ack-ack's a pretty good umbrella, keeps 'em high. *If* we're lucky . . . here comes another bugger.'

The Stuka came down, screaming into a dive. But she wasn't aiming for the *Burnside* after all. Her target was another destroyer and she hit it squarely on the stern. The destroyer was not far off *Burnside*'s port beam and the result of the hit, when the depth charges went up, was a tearing shower of metal fragments that swept like rain over *Burnside*'s upper deck, over the bridge, over the guns. Fanshawe was saved by his steel helmet, Cameron by one of the big signalling projectors. Mr Bartram was not so lucky this time but the damage was not too serious. His backside looked like a bloodbath and felt as though it was on fire and he knew he wouldn't sit down for a fortnight or more, but it could be borne. He carried on round the guns, trailing blood. There were a number of other casualties, many of them bad, and the doctor and his sick-berth staff had their hands full. Bartram counted three dead; no doubt there would be more in other parts of the ship. After a while he began to feel groggy, a little weak in the legs: he was losing too much blood. For a moment he propped himself against a guardrail and was looking towards the destroyer that had been hit when she was hit again, this time right on Number Two gun for'ard. That was the end of her; the fore magazine blew up and she went down fast, leaving bunches of men struggling in the water, black with spilled oil fuel.

On *Burnside*'s bridge the Captain was twisting his ship to port and starboard to avoid the bombs. It was largely luck, however, that kept the destroyer clear as the dive-bombers screamed down time and time again. The fighters from the carriers were not doing too well now: Cameron had seen at least eight of them spiral down into the blue water, settle for a brief moment, then vanish, sometimes with a helmeted man crawling out along a wing until his support sank beneath him. There were going to be some long faces aboard the carriers at debriefing.

But so far the convoy itself was still intact, still steaming majestically, almost uncaringly, along beneath the bursting shells. The escort was doing its job well, keeping the Germans and Italians fully occupied. *Nelson* and *Rodney* bristled like lethal hedgehogs, covering themselves and the merchant ships with a shrapnel canopy.

The gunner's mate came up behind Mr Bartram, his uniform filthy with sweat and greasy from the guns. 'You all right, sir? Stupid question—you're not! Here, I'll help you down to the wardroom.' In action, the wardroom was in use as a medical dressing station. 'Hang on to me, sir.'

'I'm all right, there's plenty worse. The doctor's got enough to worry about.'

'The sick-berth tiffy can patch you up. The bleeding's got to be stopped. We don't want to lose you, Mr Bartram. Come on now.' The gunner's mate's voice was harsh. He and Bartram got along well and the old bugger was in a bad way; when your hair began to go grey you couldn't take it quite like younger men. Just then the gunner's mate heard someone calling him, urgently, from the after 4.7-inch mounting.

'What is it?'

'Bloody misfire.'

The gunner's mate yelled back, 'Cease firing, report to the bridge. I'll be right with you.' Still holding on to Bartram, Garter looked round, tanned face grim, deeply etched with lines of worry. His eye caught a man coming aft along the upper deck and he called to him. 'You. Take Mr Bartram down to the dressing station, sharpish.'

The man doubled up; it was Leading Seaman Dewhurst. Garter gave him a hard look and said, 'Don't let him slip, all right?'

'Yes, GI.'

The gunner's mate moved aft at the rush. Dewhurst assisted Bartram towards the ladder below the after screen, went down first to act as longstop, catching some of the gunner's blood. He helped Bartram into the wardroom. The LSBA was working flat out, swabbing, bandaging. He glanced briefly at the gunner and took in the situation. He said, 'Lay him on the floor, on his side. I'll see to him soon as I can.'

Dewhurst got the gunner on the deck. Bartram said, 'Thank you, lad.' Then he passed out. Dewhurst looked round, saw some blankets, reached out for them and wedged them beneath the gunner's body to keep him from rolling back on his lacerated buttocks. Then he got to his feet and approached the LSBA.

'I'm something of a spare hand,' he said. 'I—'

'Yes. I heard.' There had been some trouble after the loss of Stripey Pond, trouble at Dewhurst's gun—a stroppy loading number who knew his job better than Dewhurst knew his, and the First Lieutenant had found it better to take Dewhurst off his action station. 'So what?'

'I can help out here,' Dewhurst said.

The LSBA stared. 'You? About as much effing use as a—'

'I can learn by watching you, can't I? Better than nothing, I'd have thought.'

'Would you? All right, then. Just watch this.'

Deftly, the LSBA applied a bandage to an upper arm badly torn by a metal sliver. Dewhurst watched closely. It was good to feel he might be wanted again.

CHAPTER FIVE

Once again the convoy and escorts made a running count of the damage and the losses: two corvettes and three destroyers sunk, the *Auckland* damaged by the fires in the earlier action, another cruiser now with her screws and rudder blown off. She was under tow of the *Nigeria*. Her guns were still intact but from now on their usefulness was going to be

66

restricted and both ships would provide slow-moving and not easily manoeuvrable targets when the enemy struck again, as he would before long. A number of other ships had sustained superficial damage along their upper decks and quite apart from the lost ships' companies the count of casualties was high: the reports to the Flag indicated 178 wounded in varying degrees and forty-one dead aboard the surviving warships. There had been some damage to the merchant ships—boats destroyed by fire when bombs had hit, funnels shredded, derricks gone—but all were watertight and seaworthy and able to steam as before. Once again, the escort had done its bit faithfully and well. Once again there was a signal from the Flag and Fanshawe broadcast it to his ship's company. *England will be proud of you*, the signal read, *and Hitler will know to his cost that the Fleet is in being still.*

'Bloody 'Itler,' Leading Seaman York said. From sheer force of habit he was rubbing up what had once, in peacetime, been brightwork around the gun-muzzles. 'I wonder why admirals is always talking pompous. 'Itler will know the effing Fleet's in being still, I ask you!' He wiped sweat from his face, using the same piece of cotton-waste he'd been using on the gun. 'Sod 'Itler.'

He was talking to the buffer, PO Burnett. Burnett said, 'It's not pompous, not really. You get like that when you have gold rings half-way

67

up your arm, it's natural.'

'Maybe. Mind, they're not all like that. I remember Sir John Kelly when 'e 'ad the flag o' the 'Ome Fleet. Never mind 'oo 'e was talking to, women an' all, he never used to ask 'em to sit down. 'E used to say, bring yer arse to an anchor. Funny old bloke, Kelly, 'ad a sense of humour. Once he ordered an evolution . . . all ships to send away a boat with the Royal Marine band embarked. They was to pull alongside the flagship playing a popular tune. Our skipper, 'e 'ad a sense of humour too. Our boat pulled alongside playing Anybody 'Ere Seen Kelly.' York gave a final wipe with his cottonwaste. ' 'Ow's the gunner getting along, eh?'

'Sore arse,' PO Burnett said briefly. 'No anchorage for a while.' He turned away and went off laughing. Bartram was going to be all right so now the funny side could be indulged in. There was always something funny about wounds to the arse, a sort of music-hall element like puffed-up blokes who slipped on banana skins. Going aft, Burnett thought about Dewhurst: he'd heard that Dewhurst had stayed in the wardroom for the rest of the action and strictly speaking that should mean a charge of leaving his place of duty in face of the enemy, since, when Dewhurst had been taken off his gun, he'd been allocated to back up the damage control parties. But no one was going to make anything of it. The Surgeon

68

Lieutenant had said Dewhurst had helped out efficiently and stopped a lot of wounds becoming worse. Maybe Dewhurst should re-muster as a po bosun.

*   *   *

There was a longish respite for no known reason. It had to be a false dawn but nevertheless the spirits of the ship's company lifted. Hitler and Musso could have been taught a lesson. Mussolini, the bullfrog of the Pontine Marshes, as Winnie had called him in one of his speeches, was all wind and piss like the barber's cat. Hit back and he collapsed. Adolf Hitler was different; smaller and thinner but much tougher. PO Pollen remarked on Hitler as he took a stand-easy in the petty officer's mess, a fag-end drooping from the corner of his mouth.

'Bloody pity someone couldn't have foretold the future when the bugger was born.'

'Eh?' the Petty Officer Telegraphist asked.

'Someone could have pulled the plug early. Aborted him from the start. Cut the whatsit, umbilical cord.'

'You always do cut that.'

'Could have cut it higher up, then. Or lower down. Just think what it would have saved. Wouldn't have been here now, would we—steaming for the effing Gap.' Pollen paused. 'Any buzzes from your cat's cradle of wire and bits of string, Sparks?'

The PO Telegraphist shrugged. 'Nothing, just the routines.'

'Useless lot, aren't you.'

'What isn't made, we don't take down, right? Anyway, we don't need buzzes. We know what's waiting for us, don't need anyone to tell us that.'

'Sure, but why are the sods holding off?'

'Nurturing their strength,' the PO Telegraphist said darkly. 'Or maybe Hitler's had a vision again, telling him to lay off. You never know your luck, eh?'

'Bloody right,' Pollen said. But something was telling him beyond doubt that they were all in for it this time and it was just a question of how many of them would see Malta. Not many, was Pollen's guess. The convoy was too bloody important and Hitler and Musso between them were going to throw in everything they'd got. Pollen was very uneasy about the present calm; just at this moment it was like the old days of peace, with the Mediterranean Fleet proceeding placidly on a cruise, showing the flag, with Admiral Sir William Fisher in charge aboard the battleship *Queen Elizabeth*. It couldn't last. Pollen, fag and stand-easy finished, left the mess and went back to the upper deck to give another PO a relieve-decks spell from first degree of readiness, maybe the last spell anyone would get for a good long while. He tried to give himself crumbs of comfort: Hitler could be chewing the odd carpet, as he was said to do when angry, or he could be grinding away in Berchtesgaden with Eva Braun and too absorbed to worry about convoys—only if he didn't, someone else would. There was no hope in that direction. Pollen shivered suddenly; it was as though the fingers of death had flicked over him. He thought of his missus and the kids, a long way off in St Ives in Huntingdonshire, a funny place for a seaman to have landed up, really. But when Pollen had left the *Andrew* a year before the war, he'd never wanted to see the hogwash again. He'd wanted a home life and for that short while, until Hitler had forced the recall of the Royal Fleet Reservists, he'd had it. It had been the best time of his life. The missus had happened to come in for a little bit of luck from her old man, who'd owned a shop in St Ives, on Market Hill, just down from the railway station and between the Red Lion and the cattle market. A bicycle shop, and he'd left it to Pollen's missus along with Pollen's mother-in-law—there always had to be a snag but he hadn't really minded. He was his own boss and doing well and then along had come bloody Hitler and his schemes. Pollen was a family-minded man, and now he was dead anxious. A couple of leaves ago a bit of carelessness had set in and another kid was due any moment. Just about the time the convoy was due to enter the Grand Harbour. If, on both counts, all went well. Evie was a little old to go through it all again.

Sod the war.

But it wouldn't, surely, touch St Ives. It was so peaceful there, sleepy—nothing ever happened. As a family they used to bicycle a lot, it was good for business for one thing. Fenstanton, Hilton, Elsworth, Conington—picnics by the river at Needingworth and the place where Hereward the Wake had crossed from the fens, Holywell. Lovely summer days, lovely green fields, the peace of rural England. All gone now. On the bridge there was unceasing vigilance. Fanshawe was there still; he had taken only one brief snatch of sleep in his sea-cabin while Williamson took over the bridge. He had slept deeply but was wide awake on the instant when Williamson, obeying his order, had had him called after one hour. He could scarcely keep his eyes open now and walked up and down his small bridge to keep himself from dropping off. Williamson had gone down to the upper deck; as ever, a First Lieutenant's time was fully occupied. Cameron was on watch and the RNR sub-lieutenant, Mackenzie, was busy at the chart table. Mackenzie, the navigator, wasn't all that *au fait* with the Mediterranean. His war service to date had been spent on North Atlantic convoys, while in peacetime he'd been Third Officer of a PSNC liner running to South America. Not that he anticipated any difficulties; a basically Merchant Service officer could cope well enough with strange waters. But he had to be very precise about the Gap. It wasn't all that wide and if action scattered the convoy he wouldn't want to put the *Burnside* on to a mine.

Nor would Fanshawe, to whom the same thought occurred at that moment. He called, 'Pilot'.

'Yes, sir?' Mackenzie brought his head and shoulders out from the chart table screen.

'The Narrows, Pilot. The minefield.'

'Yes, sir. I've been looking at it.'

'Ah—good. We don't want any slips.'

'No, sir. I don't think there'll be any.'

'Don't think, Pilot. Don't *think*—know! One cable's-length will make all the difference. We must be exact all the way through. I shall go through it with you now.' Fanshawe moved over to join Mackenzie. Two heads bent, two pencils roved over the chart, parallel rulers moved. Then Fanshawe slumped forward across the chart. His body bumped into Mackenzie's, who looked startled.

Mackenzie looked across at Cameron. 'He's gone to sleep,' he said.

Fanshawe recovered himself. He snapped, 'What was that, Pilot? Did I hear you say I'd gone to sleep?'

'I thought you had, sir.'

73

Fanshawe's face had reddened. 'Nonsense. I was not asleep, d'you hear me?'

'Yes, sir.'

'Damned impertinence to suggest I was.'

'I'm sorry, sir.'

Fanshawe started walking again, two steps one way, two the other. Cameron met Mackenzie's eye. There was danger around. An unalert captain could be as lethal to a ship as the enemy. Cameron cleared his throat and dived in at the deep end. He said, 'I believe you've overtired yourself, sir. Why not take another rest?'

'Why not shut your mouth, Cameron?'

'I'm sorry, sir. But you're nearly out on your feet and—'

'Keep silent, Cameron.'

'Sir, I—'

'That was an order. I will not be argued with. My place is here, and here I shall remain until I decide otherwise. We have been left alone too long. Another attack will come at any moment. I must be ready.'

Cameron said no more. The Captain was making excuses to himself. In Cameron's view it was criminally stupid not to take full advantage of a respite but it had to be the Captain's decision. Fanshawe was over-conscientious and he could crack at an unfortunate moment, but Cameron was able to understand his outlook. Captains always feared being caught with their pants down. All

74

the same Fanshawe was overdoing it now. His judgement had been affected.

The watch wore on; the Captain moved in a dream and Cameron believed that now and again he was falling asleep on the move. The heat wasn't helping; the sun struck down blindingly, the sea was an even brilliant blue that contrasted sharply with the white ribbons of the wakes. Along the decks, at the guns and torpedo-tubes, the seamen lay sprawled, taking it easy but ready for instant action should anything happen to break the calm. Sub-Lieutenant Mackenzie left the bridge to go below and check the master gyro. Everything had to be on top line for the passage of the Gap, which was timed for the dark hours of the next night. No slips, in Fanshawe's words, everything dead accurate.

Mackenzie watched while an electrical artificer checked circuits. He was thinking back to pre-war and the very different life aboard the PSNC's *Orellana*. Sailings from Liverpool to Rio, to the River Plate, sometimes round Cape Horn to Chilean ports. The rush and tumult of sailing day when the passengers arrived off the boat train from London, the piled baggage in the first and tourist class foyers, the gin parties in the bars, the farewells, the tears, the critical eyes of the ship's officers summing up the talent among the females. The faces that turned green when the liner left the berth, passed out from the

75

Mersey and turned to port off the Skerries to come down through St George's Channel and away across the wide ocean. As Junior Third Officer, Mackenzie had kept the twelve to four watch, twice daily, all the way out and home. That was a little restrictive to one's social life but Mackenzie had managed; there were always ways and means even though watchkeeping officers were supposed to be clear of the public rooms used by the passengers two hours before their watches started. Not all rooms were public ones; Mackenzie enjoyed himself but had steered clear of marriage. No point in a man tying himself down. Now, in wartime, he had begun to regret it; the married men had women to go back to on leave, whereas a bachelor was forever on the lookout and wasn't always lucky. Even with the laxity of war, it took time to find a bedmate, at least if you were particular, which Mackenzie was.

'All correct, sir.'

'What?'

'All correct, sir.' There was a grin on the EA's face; the lower deck was not unaware of the sub's shore-side adventures or of his resulting preoccupations.

'Oh—sorry. Thanks. Well, that's that, then.' Mackenzie returned the grin. He had spent his last ten-day leave in Glasgow, unconstructively. During it he had happened to run into EA Evans, whose home was in the

76

Gorbals. A democratically minded officer, Mackenzie had had a drink with Evans in a pub in Sauchiehall Street. They'd had rather a lot of whiskies and chasers and Mackenzie had approached a girl sitting by herself in a corner. Mackenzie should have been warned off by the fact that there were two chairs at the table and that under the empty one was a blue Burberry raincoat. Mackenzie had been chatting up the girl and getting a cold response when a lieutenant-commander RN had come back from the gents. Mackenzie had made a rapid retreat, with apologies. A moment later, rejoining the EA, he had heard the loud, acid comment:

'What can you expect of officers who drink with ratings?'

An embarrassing moment. Evans, a man of tact, had got up and left quickly.

Mackenzie climbed back to the upper deck. Malta lay ahead; perhaps it would bring better luck. Mackenzie never lost hope and each new port was a challenge. For him, Malta was virgin territory, however inappropriate the adjective might be.

*   *   *

During the afternoon watch signals came from the Flag, quite a number of them. The Admiral had been pondering with his staff officers and conferring by lamp with the Rear-

Admiral Aircraft-Carrier Squadron. So far there had been no indication either from the radar or from the reconnaissance aircraft to confirm that the Italian battlefleet was lurking ahead. This did not mean they were not somewhere in the vicinity. The convoy's strategy had to be based upon the presumption they were there—fast, heavily gunned battleships and cruisers. It was said in the British Fleet that the Italians carried most of their guns aft, which was handier for running away, but this was not to be taken too seriously. There was puzzlement in the Admiral's mind as to why no further aerial attack had developed and he was offering no guesses other than to suggest to his commanding officers that the enemy was biding his time for the grand assault. It behoved them all to be extra vigilant for a surprise attack by U-boats or Italian submarines. The latter were known to be roving: Mussolini still believed in the concept of *Mare Nostrum*—and not without some reason. None of the earlier Malta convoys had been easy to fight through and the losses had been very heavy—hence the state of siege, and the terrible depletion of food stocks. Not all of this was contained in the signals from the Flag, but all of it was inherent in them, as Fanshawe knew.

He sent for his First Lieutenant.

'We must be ready for anything, Number

One. I take the point that I know you're about to make—that we always are. That may be so. But this time I want to be extra certain. I want all aspects of our fighting capacity and our *survival* capacity checked once again. A special reference to damage control and an overhaul of the boats and Carley floats.'

'Aye, aye, sir,' Williamson said. There was nothing else he could say; you couldn't tell the Captain he was approaching pedantry. Another check was utterly pointless but now it had to be made. When the word reached the buffer, PO Burnett, he scratched his head and muttered profanities. As if there wasn't enough to do. However, as a long service man, a Fleet Reservist like Pollen, he'd seen it all before. Some skippers went berserk over manoeuvres, the annual peacetime jamboree between the combined Home and Mediterranean Fleets when they used to assemble in Gibraltar and try to score points off each other. A skipper's promotion depended a lot on how his ship performed in mock war and they were all dead keen, even those whose private means made the extra pay attendant upon rank look like chickenfeed. They all wanted to fly their flags as admirals one day. There was nothing quite like being an admiral in the pre-war Navy; if a captain was God, then only God knew what an admiral ranked as. The whole trinity, presumably. One stripe for each of them with another broad

79

gold band to represent the archangels . . .

'Sod it,' Burnett said, feeling fed up to the back teeth. He went round the upper deck, disturbing seamen snatching a bit of kip while they could. He got hold of the captains of the fo'c'sle, iron deck and quarterdeck and delegated his responsibilities. PO Pollen shrugged his shoulders philosophically and obeyed orders, poking and probing, checking the boats' bags and compasses, the iron rations, the falls and the disengaging gear, the ditching apparatus for the Carley floats. Everything was in order except for just one thing, and the buffer was with Pollen when he found it. The ship's cat, Beano, was ensconced in the sternsheets of the motor-boat along with a litter of six.

Burnett was scandalized. 'Bloody Beano. Wonder when *that* got done! Bloody cover must have been loose and that's your responsibility, Jack. Have 'em out pronto.'

Pollen scratched his head. 'Where am I going to put 'em, eh?'

'I don't know,' Burnett said, 'and I don't care. Somewhere safe, poor little buggers. That's if any of us are safe which we bloody aren't. There's just one thing.'

'Yes?'

'Try to keep it from the bridge. Once the skipper knows, he'll go berserk round the entire ship. He'll want the hands piped to Quarters Clean Guns and clean every bloody thing else into the bargain.'

In fact the news went round the ship like lightning. It was regarded as a good omen. Beano, she wouldn't produce without believing the little buggers had a good chance. Beano was a real ship's cat, herself born aboard the *Burnside* in a Force Eight gale in the Western Ocean while the destroyer had been engaged in action with a U-boat. She not only had her sea legs from the start but her first breath of air had been full of gunsmoke. She knew what she was about, according to Leading Seaman York. York, who wasn't especially fond of cats as a species, preferring dogs, had a soft spot for Beano, the only one of her mum's litter that had survived. The rest had gone overboard, skittering willy-nilly across the iron deck when a sea had broken the wash-deck locker adrift, the place that had been their maternity home. Beano had fetched up against York's seaboot and he'd scooped her up and carried her below to the messdeck. Soon after that, fortunately weaned, she had become an orphan, her mother being run over by a lorry during a spell in Londonderry. Dad had probably been around somewhere in the UK but that wasn't much help. Beano had become York's special friend but even he hadn't noticed that she'd become pregnant. Now, with the problem passed to him by PO Pollen, he was at his wits' end to know what to do about the litter. It was a fine thing, slap in the

81

middle of a Malta convoy.

Help, however, came from an unexpected source: Leading Seaman Dewhurst. Dewhurst liked cats, all cats, not just Beano. Diffidently he approached York. He said, 'I'll see to them if you like. I've got—'

'Piss off,' York said.

'If you'll just listen,' Dewhurst said doggedly. 'I've got—'

'Bollocks. You'll go an' lose 'em overboard. You're too bloody cack-handed to be true, *Mister* Dewhurst.' York was still obsessed with the impertinence of Dewhurst thinking he could ever have been an officer. Nevertheless, something had to be done about the kittens. If the skipper got to know and couldn't be reassured that they'd not be a perishing nuisance, he might go and order them to be drowned which was what most people did with kittens anyway, let alone in the middle of the Med at war. So York decided to cool it. Grudgingly he said, 'Well, *what* have you got?' Suddenly, light dawned. Dewhurst's mother, confident that sonny boy would get his commission, had bought him a lovely pansy officer's suitcase, best leather, which, ever since Dewhurst had come aboard, had been a flaming bloody nuisance in the hammock netting at the after end of the seamen's messdeck. Dewhurst nursed it like a baby, standing guard whenever hammocks were shifted in the netting. 'That suitcase?' York asked.

'Yes.'

'Blow me down with a fart. You know what them kittens'll do in it, don't you?'

'Of course I do. I can line it with cotton-waste. I'll look after them well, don't worry.'

York looked at him sardonically. 'Cut 'oles in it for air?'

'No. I'll find a way round that.'

'Uh-huh.' Reflectively, York rubbed at his chin. 'Well, all right, then. And thanks. But if you lose any I'll do you, understand?'

Dewhurst nodded. He looked happier than he'd looked for quite a while. Leading Seaman i/c Kittens might not be much of a title but it was something he could do and it might get him on better terms along the messdeck. Seamen were always soft about ships' cats and these kittens, arriving when they had, were going to be more than mascots. Beano would have to be coddled. Dewhurst brought out the suitcase and settled them in. Beano purred loudly. Life was fine, very exclusive, what better could you get than an officers' pattern suitcase?

A little before the swift fall of the Mediterranean dark Leading Seaman Dewhurst was given permission from the PO of the damage control party to nip below for two minutes, no more. He brought some tinned milk from the galley store and fed it to Beano along with some baked beans which were rejected. The suitcase was now situated in the galley flat, aft of the clamped-down door into the messdeck. No one wanted Beano and family to risk drowning behind the watertight bulkhead if the fo'c'sle should be hit.

As Beano's pink tongue tested the tinned milk the first of the action signals was flashed by a blue-shaded lamp from the Flag: units of the Italian battlefleet had been picked up on the *Nelson*'s radar. They were twenty miles ahead and closing at high speed.

CHAPTER SIX

'This is it,' Fanshawe said. He was busy with his binoculars, scanning the dark horizon ahead of the convoy, waiting for something to show. 'Cameron?'

'Sir?'

'Tell the ship's company.'

Fanshawe didn't want to take his eyes away. Cameron moved to the tannoy and clicked on. He said, 'This is the bridge. *Nelson*'s raised the Italian Fleet ahead. Action is expected to commence within six minutes—the combined closing speed is estimated at thirty-nine knots. The guns will not open in quarters firing until orders are passed from the bridge.'

He switched off. There was a curious silence, a tense silence broken only by the ship noises and the sigh of water past the hull. There was a lot of phosphorescent light from the wakes, green swathes eerily cutting the darkness. The escort was well spaced out, the leading ships some miles ahead of the rearguard. The merchant ships were great dark shadows, keeping station well. Aboard the *British Racer* Captain Harcourt sent up a prayer that the massive armament of the *Nelson* and the *Rodney* would keep the Italians off. The battleships had increased speed and were moving ahead to take the brunt. Harcourt knew very well what the end would be for his officers and men if the smallest shell should penetrate his tanks: instant oblivion for the lucky ones, a dreadful, unthinkable agony for those who didn't die fast. The same with the armament supply ships. Captain Harcourt thought about his son. It would go hard with him if anything should happen to the *Burnside*, if his son should be lost. He felt a personal responsibility: over many years he had influenced Hugh towards the sea. That could have been a wrong thing to do, but the sea had been his life and he could think of no better for his son. The sea was hard but it bred men, and there was much satisfaction in command. Now he had landed Hugh in this; but after all it was war. The boy would have been called up in any case. Might have found himself in the Army, might have gone at Dunkirk. And all said and done, the sea services had a much more comfortable time of it than the troops in the field.

Like Fanshawe, like all the commanding officers, Harcourt was staring ahead, probing the darkness to find the enemy, standing by to take such instant avoiding action as might be possible when things started happening.

The first any of them saw was a blue flashing lamp from the destroyer in the lead of the convoy: *Enemy in sight.* A moment later, after a pause that could be described as pregnant, the 16-inch guns opened from *Nelson* and *Rodney.* The scene was brought alive with the flashes and the roar of the charges as eighteen gun-muzzles sent the high-explosive shells flinging intermittently towards the Italians.

*   *   *

The noise of the pounding was intense, unimaginable to those who hadn't heard it before. The constant flashes lit the silhouettes of the battleships, giving them the awesome appearance of black mammoths ringed with fire. Huge spouts of water rose on the convoy's flanks as the enemy hit back. So far, the Italian gunners hadn't got the deflection, though the ranging seemed to be spot on.

On *Burnside's* bridge the personnel stood like statues: Fanshawe, Cameron, Sub-Lieutenant Coulter in charge of the Asdics,

Mackenzie, together with the leading signalman now acting as yeoman, and the lookouts to port and starboard. There was nothing to do at this stage but wait. Already the convoy had broadened its line of advance, spreading out on orders from the Commodore, and the escort had also been deployed farther out so as to diversify the target. The aircraft-carriers with their attendant destroyers were like great skyscrapers above the others as they turned into such wind as could be raised in order to fly off their squadrons. Cameron watched the mass take-off as the big guns continued to give intermittent light. Soon shore-based torpedo-bombers joined in the attack, coming in low across the water to drop their tin fish before lifting and turning away from the anti-aircraft barrage. Some distance off *Burnside*'s port bow a brilliant flash came, a flash that blossomed into a sheet of flame tinged with black smoke that stood clearly visible as it wreathed back across the flame. The acting yeoman of signals reported in a voice that betrayed his tension, '*Argyll*, sir!'

Wordlessly Fanshawe nodded. He stared through his glasses. *Argyll*, a 9,400-ton heavy cruiser carrying twelve 6-inch guns and eight 4-inch AA armament, would be a serious loss if she was put out of action. The fires were spreading, the flames licking up from aft. Aboard her were eight hundred men, but better not to think about that. Fanshawe swallowed, felt a looseness starting in his stomach. Then, not far off *Burnside*'s port beam, one of the ammunition ships went up. One moment she was there, steaming on, a dark shadow moving through the green phosphorescent glow of her bow-wave and wake, carrying some forty men and 10,000 tons of explosive war material, The next she had vanished under a spreading plume of fire and thick, acrid smoke. The explosion rocked the destroyer, seeming to send her broadside through the water to starboard.

Fanshawe, clinging fast to the binnacle, said, 'God above.'

'Scrambling nets, sir?'

'For what, Cameron?'

'Some of the bridge personnel may have been blown clear, sir.'

Fanshawe didn't bother to respond. He stared in awe, horrified at the sudden obliteration, the total nothingness that was left behind. No one could possibly have survived. Fanshawe and Cameron, all those on the bridge, scanned the area with their binoculars. Fire and smoke rolled outwards and there was no sign of life beyond its fringe. As *Burnside* steamed on with the convoy even the fires died down: there was nothing left to burn apart from the spilled fuel oil bunkers. The ship had simply fragmented along with her crew. Before *Burnside* had moved clear some of the debris had fallen shatteringly along her upper deck.

The First Lieutenant made an inspection: a number of Carley floats had been pierced, the funnels were riddled and engine fumes were escaping through a number of small holes. The decks and upperworks were pitted and scarred and there had been many casualties at the guns and all other exposed places. Four men had died. One of them was Petty Officer Bunney, captain of the fo'c'sle. Williamson found him at the foot of the ladder running down from the break of the fo'c'sle to the iron deck, with a jagged piece of steel where his adam's-apple had been. Williamson knelt, saw there was no life, and stood up to find Leading Seaman York staring down.

'Dead, sir?'

'Yes.'

'Poor old Bunney, eh. 'E was on top line for Chief PO. I reckon—' York broke off. The destroyer had heeled sharply and signals were coming from Rear-Admiral(D) in the flotilla leader. Williamson climbed the ladders to the bridge, where he reported the state of the upper deck to the Captain.

Fanshawe nodded. He said, 'I've been ordered to stand by the *Argyll* with *Burgoyne* and *Brahmin*. *Argyll's* been hit by a torpedo aft. All four shafts out of action.'

The First Lieutenant's lips framed an unuttered whistle: to lie stopped in the middle of an action was no one's idea of joy. As the destroyer turned back on her course more signals were made by lamp from the Commodore of the convoy: he was about to execute a 180-degree turn to starboard, taking the merchant ships and the close escort of destroyers farther from the Italian guns while the battleships and cruisers engaged and acted as a shield. The three destroyers detailed to stand by the *Argyll* received more orders from the flotilla leader: the crippled cruiser was to be taken in tow and then brought to rejoin the convoy and its destroyer screen.

Fanshawe said, 'Stand by to tow aft, Number One.'

'Aye, aye, sir.' Williamson clattered down the ladder and went aft to the quarterdeck, shouting for PO Pollen. As he did so there were more cataclysmic explosions among the turning convoy. Two more ships had been hit; one of them a supply ship, the other one of the liners crammed with troops. Williamson saw the liner ringed with fire, the centre of the blaze being the bridge. She must have been hit by a shell from one of the Italian battleships, a shell that would have driven right down through her passenger decks. As Williamson watched, the aerial attacks began again from the shore-based aircraft. The convoy wasn't to be given any chance at all. Once more the signalling started up, bringing fresh orders from Rear-Admiral(D): *Burnside* and her consorts were to move in to pick up survivors from the troopship. The *Argyll* would have to wait.

*   *   *

PO Garter had a feeling that they were not going to come through. He wouldn't be seeing the Gut again. Hitler and Musso were going to make a job of this and as a result it would be all up with Malta—island, as they said in the Fleet, of priests, goats, bells and smells, very descriptive. Garter had had some good times in Malta, having in his day spent two full commissions with the Mediterranean Fleet. Valletta was all right and never mind the description. Women and drink, not quite free but a darn sight less costly than in the home ports. With some exceptions that was: not long ago in Londonderry Garter had been approached by a ponce outside a pub. Just as a matter of interest Garter had enquired the price of the goods offered. Sixpence the man had said, sixpence for a quick job in a dark alley. Garter had expressed amazement; the man, misinterpreting the reason for his astonishment, had gone on to explain that since the start of the war the price had had to go up. When Garter got back aboard, no one had believed him. Garter had often wondered just what he would have got for the sixpence. Even in Malta it wasn't that cheap. Now, they were no doubt doing it for food or fags, both of which would be more valuable than any

God's amount of money. Sieges were very nasty things to live through. Garter very much wanted to get the convoy in and sucks to Musso; but there was still that morbid feeling. Not all the bull of peacetime, not all the gate-and-gaiters shouting of Whale Island-trained gunner's mates, was going to be enough. If the forces ranged against you were superior, then you'd had it. That was the long and short of it. If only the bloody politicians had listened earlier to Winston Churchill, and made some proper effort to rearm instead of piddling about with the problem. There were never enough escorts and most of the capital ships were as old as Garter's aunt. They dated back to the last lot. Been at Jutland, most of them. As for *Nelson* and *Rodney*, they hadn't the speed, the Eyeties could steam rings round them if they chose to. They couldn't even fire a full broadside. *Nelson* had tried it on gunnery trials when she was new, all nine 16-inch together. Result, the fo'c'sle had split from elbow to breakfast time. Since that, both ships had been forced to restrict their broadsides to two turrets and fire the third one separately. What a way, Garter thought, to build a navy. The politicians again—*Nelson* and *Rodney* had been buggered up on the stocks, cut to something like half size on account of the Washington treaty. Hitler had cocked a snook at all that and gone ahead with full-scale rearmament. So had Musso. And now they were seeing the result. Some people never learned. Like Ordinary Seaman Fison, who chose this moment to waylay the gunner's mate with a complaint.

Ordinary Seaman Fison hadn't had his supper.

'Bugger off,' Garter said briefly.

'But it's not—'

'If you haven't had your bloody supper, you've had your time. All hands got relieve decks before the Eyeties came up. Any deficiencies in your gut is your own bloody fault, all right?'

'All thc same, I want to state—'

Garter's voice rose. 'You'll state nothing, got that? Any man that thinks of his perishing feed when other men are dying, he's just bloody rotten. Shop steward before you were conscripted—right?'

'Yes.'

'I don't know what your bloody union was and I don't care. At a guess, Union of Mannequins in a French letter factory. If you don't piss off pronto, back to your station, my lad, you'll be in the union of ratings on a charge of leaving your place of duty in face of the enemy. For that, you get death.'

Garter pushed him aside and went on aft. He reached the quarterdeck just as the Stukas came in. One of them made a personal dive attack on the *Burnside*. Garter watched the bombs fall, watched the tracer going up—

going up and making no impression. The bombs missed, but were close enough to send waterspouts over the deck and make the ship ring like a bell from the shock of the explosions. Then the Stuka came in again, this time a raking machine-gun attack. Garter saw the First Lieutenant go down in a heap, and ran towards him. He was alive, just; but he hadn't long to go. Breath rattled in his throat and frothy blood came from the mouth. He died in Garter's arms, before the gunner's mate could get a message to the doctor. Garter let the head go back to the deck. He'd have to stay there for now. No time for the niceties, the war had to be got on with.

*   *   *

The three destroyers approached the rim of oil-covered sea that surrounded the sinking troopship. Fanshawe's thought was what it had been all along, the same as Cameron had felt at the start: troopships shouldn't be part of a supply convoy, they shouldn't be kept down to the speed of the slower vessels; but he had to acknowledge that his own war experience had been confined to the North Atlantic and that the Med was different. It was a confined sea; and everything, fast and slow alike, had to converge on the Narrows between Sicily and Tunisia. But it was still a tragedy. The liner had been carrying around five thousand men—an infantry brigade with its attached guns and transport and headquarters staff bound for the Middle East together with some detachments to be landed at Malta as replacements. Many would have died when the shell drove through the crowded decks. Many more were going to die if and when the order came from the Master to abandon ship.

That order must come within the next few minutes.

Sub-Lieutenant Coulter came up to report the scrambling nets over the side and the seaboat's crew in their boat with the lowerers standing by. He had something else to report as well.

'First Lieutenant's been killed, sir.'

Fanshawe stared, wiping sweat and dirt from his face. 'That's bad,' he said inadequately. What else was there to say? He turned to Cameron as the destroyer moved in for the liner; by now the heat of the fire could be felt, searingly. Debris lay scattered on the water, burning where the fuel spillage took it. No men yet. Fanshawe said, 'You heard that, Cameron. You know what it means. You're the next senior.'

Cameron said, 'Yes, sir.' He was, as of the moment Williamson had died, the First Lieutenant. It would be a big responsibility, but it wasn't the moment to think about that. The next report came from the starboard lookout in the bridge wing.

'Men in the water, sir, starboard.'

Fanshawe picked them up in his binoculars. Fire licked round them; they had probably swum submerged for as far as they could manage and had come up too soon. They were going to fry.

Fanshawe said, 'Away seaboat's crew. Wait a moment. Cameron, you've had experience in taking boats away.'

'Yes, sir.'

'I want you to take over. Bring off all you can. Coulter, you'll take over the watch.'

CHAPTER SEVEN

Under Cameron's charge the seaboat was pulled towards the circle of fire. The heat grew more and more intense. Exposed skin felt scorched. Soon the liner's boats were seen, moving through the smoke from the sinking ship, crammed to capacity with soldiers, the woodwork taking fire as the flames licked. From the water more men reached out, holding fast to ropes looped along the sides of the lifeboats and being pulled along with them.

'All right, York,' Cameron said to his coxswain. 'Take her in. Over there.' He pointed away to port. 'There's some heads. Let's hope we're in time, that's all!'

The seaboat's crew pulled. Handled expertly

by Leading Seaman York, she headed fast for the struggling group. Flames came up the sides; the air was stifling now, with an overpowering stench of oil fuel and of burning flesh. Bodies floated past, their clothing alight in the sea of oil. As the boat came up to its target Cameron passed the order to lay on oars, then to ship oars. Hands reached out and badly burned men were brought inboard, some of them screaming. The sound tore at Cameron's nerves. Some of them were not going to live, others were going to be scarred for life. It was a wonder that any at all among the swimmers had survived. When he had taken all he could, Cameron brought his burning boat away and as soon as they were clear the flames were dealt with. Back alongside the destroyer, the seaboat was hooked on to the falls and hoisted so that the burned men could be lifted out as gently as possible and taken below to the medical dressing station in the wardroom. Leading Seaman Dewhurst was at the falls, taking charge. He looked away when he caught York's eye, but York had no criticism to offer. Dewhurst was doing all right. Away to the east, the thunder of the battleship's guns could be heard and there were more explosions and orange-coloured fires as more ships, as yet unnamed, were hit.

Fanshawe was on the loud hailer, shouting aft. 'Cameron!'

'Sir?'

'Get back in again as soon as the survivors are out.'

'Aye, aye, sir.' It was probably useless by now but you couldn't give up while there was a chance of one life being saved, one man's agony assuaged by the morphine in the doctor's charge. Once again the seaboat was slipped; Cameron saw the boats going in from *Burgoyne* and *Brahmin*, their crews pulling like galley-slaves of old. The liner's boats were now making up alongside the three destroyers, discharging their loads. As Cameron moved back into the flaming oil, the liner settled finally, her back breaking and bow and stern lifting for a while before they slid back beneath the sea. There was a dull explosion, a roar of steam, and the water boiled up in tumult. There were no more men to be picked up. Only bodies now.

Cameron took the seaboat back to the falls.

*   *   *

At 0200 hours next morning the Italian fleet hauled off to the east, pursued by the guns of the *Nelson* and the *Rodney*. The convoy and escort licked their wounds. The Admiral reported three enemy cruisers sunk and heavy damage sustained by the Italian battleships, though not enough to sink them. Of the merchant ships, four had gone: the troopship and the armament carrier, together with two of the vessels carrying foodstuffs for Malta. Two cruisers and four destroyers of the escort had been blown up; the *Argyll* still lay crippled but was now being taken in tow by destroyers detached from the close escort after *Burnside* and her two consorts had been withdrawn and ordered in to pick up survivors.

The Admiral signalled: *so much for the Italian fleet*.

Fanshawe smiled wryly and said, 'There's still a long way to go to Malta. When we reach the Narrows we'll have the E boats coming in.'

'And the Stukas again,' Cameron said.

'Yes. You'd better have a count of casualties, Number One, and reorganize the guns' crews. Get together with Mr Bartram and the gunner's mate.'

'What about you, sir?'

'I'm all right.'

Cameron said, 'You need sleep, sir.'

'Perhaps. But it's not possible yet. After dawn—then I'll see.'

Cameron went down the ladder, leaving the RNR sub on watch. He carried out a detailed inspection of the ship above and below, accompanied by the gunner, the coxswain and the buffer. The casualties, though bad enough as were all casualties, had not in fact been heavy: six men dead including the First Lieutenant, eighteen wounded by the flying debris when the ammunition ship had gone.

Apart from the damage caused at the same time to the Carley floats, and the peppering of the funnels, *Burnside* was shipshape and intact. When Cameron went below to the engine-room, he found everything proceeding with its normal calm, if calm was the word for the engine spaces. Mr Canton, in clean white overalls, reported no difficulties.

'Just that perishing seepage,' he said, 'and even that's under control, Mr Cameron.'

'Those near misses—'

'Oh, yes, they gave me a moment's thought. Nothing more.' Canton grinned. 'Takes a bloody sight more'n that to upset one of His Majesty's engine-rooms!'

Cameron went on his way. Canton watched him climb the network of steel ladders with his retinue. The Chief tilted his uniform cap back on his head and scratched reflectively. The Executive Branch, the seaman officers, they couldn't move without assistance. Like the top brass in hospitals—doctor's rounds. Mr Canton remembered countless Captain's Rounds aboard battleships and cruisers. Every Saturday forenoon ... Captain, Commander, Surgeon Commander, Commander(E), Paymaster Commander, First Lieutenant, Divisional Officers, Gunnery Lieutenant, Torpedo Lieutenant, this-that-and-the-other Lieutenant ... Master-at-Arms, Regulating Petty Officers, bugler, sideboys and messengers. Normally the Captain would wear a clean pair of white gloves and if, when he ran his gloved fingers along some obscure length of lagged piping below decks, that glove was seen to be ever so slightly dusty, then the Commander got hell and passed it back along the line until eventually the whole load of crap landed on some poor bloody leading hand. By being in the engine-room branch you escaped some of the bull. You werc also worse off in action. You might not get sliced up by metal fragments or shrapnel but if the ship took a shell or a tin fish in the engine-room or boiler-room then you'd had it. No hope, or very little. Also, if the ship went down at all suddenly, you couldn't just slide over into the drink.

Not that there was any bull about young Cameron, Mr Canton went on to reflect as he pondered on the Executive Branch. He was RNVR and not only that, he was wartime RNVR, ex-lower deck. The RNVR came in two varieties: pre-war and wartime. Some of the pre-war ones thought they were more RN that the Dartmouth products ... gentlemen with experience of yachting. Stone the crows, Mr Canton thought, the *Andrew* wasn't a collection of perishing yachts piddling about the Solent! Give him the Cameron sort, every time. He wondered how Cameron would make out now he was acting Jimmy.

*　　　*　　　*

101

In addition to the wardroom, the officers' cabins had now been taken over for the accommodation of the badly burned men among the survivors. The less badly burned, bandaged by the medical staff assisted by Leading Seaman Dewhurst, kipped down where they could. *Burnside* began to look like a hospital ship, all white and lint-pink with a smell of antiseptic overlying the normal ship smells of oil and hot metal, rope and the contents of the boatswain's store. Dewhurst was enjoying his self-imposed role, a role that seemed to have been accepted by the coxswain and the new First Lieutenant. The burned soldiers needed him and he responded. They treated him virtually as a doctor; his public school accent helped to gain him a touch of authority. In between times he was fulfilling his promise to York and looking after Beano and her litter, still dossing down in his leather suitcase outside the galley.

Dawn came up. As the sun rose higher, brilliant in a clear blue sky, Fanshawe reduced the ship to second degree of readiness. One watch could get some sleep. For now, the enemy had gone. Most of the hands crashed down where they had been standing; when the Eyeties and the Nazis returned, they preferred to be on deck. The attack would come suddenly, from out of the sun if it was to be by air, and no one liked being caught below. Those whose station in action was below were

102

plain unlucky.

Fanshawe said, 'Take over, Number One. I'm going to my sea-cabin. Call me in accordance with standing orders.' He moved away, stiffly, like an automaton that had been over-wound. He would take time to relax into a refreshing sleep; his mind would still be active, going over and over what he should do in any imaginable set of circumstances. That was a captain's duty: decision, to be instant, had to be well rehearsed.

Cameron turned to the Officer of the Watch, Mackenzie. He said, 'Go and get some sleep, Sub. The Mid can take over—right, Harcourt?'

'Yes, sir.'

Mackenzie handed over the watch and went off gratefully, after a quick look at the chart. He would have to be back on the bridge at noon to take a sun sight and fix the ship's position as per daily routine. Just after he had gone, the Surgeon Lieutenant came up to the bridge.

'Where's Father?' he asked.

'Sea-cabin.'

'About time—I'm glad to hear it. Will he want my report, or do we leave him? I advise the latter, but you know what he is.'

Cameron smiled, a weary smile; he was dead tired himself. 'I'll take it for now, Doc. No doubt he'll want to see you later.'

Fleming nodded and made his report;

everything was in good hands but some of the worse burned of the soldiers were not going to make it into Malta. 'Probably better for them if they don't,' Fleming said sombrely. 'Some of them . . . God, they're barely recognizable as humans! I've seen it before, of course, in casualty. But never so many all at once. It's given me a wrench, you know.'

Cameron nodded sympathetically. 'How's Dewhurst bearing up?' he asked.

'Very well. Very useful. Hardly a seaman's job, of course. How long can I keep him?'

Cameron shrugged. 'As long as Father wears it. He's better employed with you than doing something that might be dangerous in action.'

'It can't go on for ever, though. What about that charge?' Fleming had dropped his voice; the bridge lookouts were within earshot if they should listen. 'Is it going to be dropped, or what?'

'I don't know. It's up to the Captain, Doc. He'll have it in mind, you can be sure of that. We may land him in Malta—but I really don't know.' In an almost automatic movement Cameron brought his glasses up to his eyes and examined the sky and the horizons. Nothing hostile around. But no one could relax for a moment when they carried the responsibility of the ship and its part in the escort. Fleming went below, back to his duties; there would be no relaxation for him either until the ship berthed in the Grand Harbour or

Sliema Creek and the wounded men could be discharged ashore to Bighi Hospital.

Cameron lowered his glasses, then lifted them again on the ships of the convoy. '*British Racer*'s all shipshape,' he remarked to the midshipman.

'Yes, sir.'

Cameron saw Harcourt bend and touch a finger to the wooden grating below the gyro repeater. Superstition ... but Cameron rather wished he hadn't said what he had. Everybody who went down to the sea in ships had some superstition in their make-up. Stupid things: you never whistled aboard a ship unless you wanted wind. You didn't kill an albatross, repository of the souls of mariners dead and gone. If, inadvertently, you made a glass ring when you were having a drink, you stopped it immediately; if you didn't, then a sailor's death would result. Many others, all dating back to the old sailing Navy, the days when ships were wood and men were made of iron. Captain Harcourt would very likely remember those days; the merchant ships had carried sail, or many of them had, for years after the RN had turned wholly over to steam.

Cameron asked the question. 'Was your father trained in sail, Mid?'

'Yes. Square rig.'

'Round Cape Horn?'

Harcourt nodded. 'Several times, as an apprentice and second mate.'

'Both ways—east and west? Both feet on the wardroom table?'

The midshipman grinned; he had understood the reference. To have taken advantage of the privilege might have been unmannerly, but officers who had done both passages of the dreaded Horn were entitled to recline with their feet firmly lifted to the table. There were none left in the RN now, though there were still senior officers around who had done their early cadet training aboard the old sailing line-of-battleship *Britannia* moored out in the stream off what was to become the Royal Naval College at Dartmouth. Different days ... days of climbing out along lofted yards, of gnarled old petty officer instructors whose fathers might just have sailed as boys under Lord Nelson, days of dirks and bumfreezers and rows of brass buttons, days when seamanship was paramount in the life of a young naval officer and the guns were a necessary evil whose firing shattered both peace and paintwork, days when crusted admirals and captains afloat had the cables of the Fleet burnished each time they were used and all too often destroyed the efficiency of the watertight doors of the steel ships by having them burnished as well. Those days had held bad as well as good; but both before them and since them the British Fleet had moved supreme about its business on these same Mediterranean waters, carrying the flag of

Empire and enforcing the Pax Britannica.

This morning the peace, the temporary respite, was broken by Mr Bartram. The gunner came to the bridge, looking worried. Cameron said, 'Now what's up, Guns?'

'Leading Seaman Tasker, sir. Gone sick—told to, didn't want to. He's a good hand.'

'What's the trouble?'

'Poisoned arm. Cut by a splinter and didn't report it. Turned septic it has—nasty. Dirty red line creeping up to the armpit and he can hardly move it.'

'I see. So?'

Bartram said, 'I need a replacement on Number Four gun mounting, that's what. I've no other gunnery rate available, but we *do* have a leading hand that's had some sort of experience.'

'Dewhurst?'

Bartram nodded. 'Right. Dewhurst as ever was.'

'It's essential? No—don't tell me, I know—it is.'

'Yes. Bloody pity but there we are. Can I have him back from the sick bay?'

'I suppose you'll have to, Guns. Any port in a storm. But he'll have to watch it. No more cock-ups.'

'I'll put a little stiffening in him,' Bartram said, sounding grim. 'Or my GI will.' He turned away and left the bridge. The convoy moved on steadily. Bartram had a word with the coxswain and then with the doctor. After that, when Dewhurst reported as ordered, the gunner's mate took him aside. 'Now then. You're detailed back to a leading rate's job on Number Four. In action stations, that is. You'll take charge as captain of the gun, right? I know you 'aven't the non-sub rating but we 'ave to make do. If you make a balls of it I'll 'ave you. All understood?'

'What about those troops, GI?' Dewhurst was obvious in his reluctance.

'They'll be all right. Got to be. There's a war on, sonny! You'll be bloody fighting it.'

Dewhurst swallowed, fidgeted. Any excuse . . . with a touch of desperation he said, 'There's Beano.'

The gunner's mate's dark-jowled face, flushed now, was thrust close to Dewhurst's. 'Fuck the cat. I never in all my service thought I'd 'ear drivel like that! God give me strength to endure purgatory.'

*   *   *

Away ahead of the convoy and the advanced destroyer screen a faint, virtually unnoticeable kefuffle disturbed the water, making a feather of spray. Very briefly; then it was gone. The submarine remained at periscope depth but with the periscope itself now withdrawn back into its housing. The submarine was Italian; and its captain was congratulating himself on a slice of luck. There had been a fault of navigation and he had no business to be where he was—but Il Duce would never castigate him if he managed to sink some ships of the great convoy. True, attacks were best mounted during the dark hours; but he had no intention of passing up such an opportunity. He was at extreme range, very possibly out of range of the British Asdics, but the convoy was moving on to an excellent bearing for attack and if he fired off all his torpedoes—well, he could scarcely miss with them all. Having fired them, he would immediately go deep down and scuttle away safely. There was so little risk; and so much honour and fame waiting afterwards. He would be fêted in Rome, and after the fêting would come the promotion and the decoration, and there would be Francesca, wife of the impotent Duke of Tuscany, who had always appreciated a real man. The torpedoes would be fired off in her name.

CHAPTER EIGHT

On the bridge with Harcourt, Cameron saw the flag hoist from the Commodore at the same time as the leading signalman, who reported, 'Submarine attack starboard, sir!'

Cameron lost no time in wondering why no submarine had been picked up by the advanced Asdics: he pressed the button for the alarm rattlers and the ship resounded to their urgent racket. Fanshawe came out from his sea-cabin, fully dressed and ready. Throughout the ship the men who had been stood down doubled back to their stations. In the rush and tumble through the galley flat, the slightly propped-open lid of Dewhurst's suitcase came down, imprisoning Beano and her kittens. The pathetic mew was unheard. From the medical dressing station Leading Seaman Dewhurst went aft to his gun, filled with misgivings. On the bridge signals were read off from the Flag, indicating the sighting of more torpedo trails weaving into the convoy.

On orders from Rear-Admiral(D), the destroyers on the convoy's starboard flank were deployed to search and kill the attacking submarine. *Burnside*, *Burgoyne* and *Brahmin* were ordered to remain with the convoy but to move up to starboard and act as close escort.

Soon after this a torpedo was observed on the surface, moving very slowly. Then another, and another ... they had all reached the end of their run; they lay helpless, wallowing, waiting for the opening of the automatic valves that would admit water into the main bodies and cause them to sink. No more trails were sighted; plainly, there was just the one submarine in the vicinity and she had now fired off her full load. A degree of relaxation mixed with cheerful, derisive laughter had set in when the *British Racer* was seen to be dropping astern and slewing off course, while a number of men were seen running aft to stare down over her counter. Soon she began signalling to the Commodore. Within the minute details of the *British Racer*'s predicament were being sent to the Flag, and the Flag relayed them to the ships of the escort.

Aboard *Burnside* the leading signalman took down the message and reported to the Captain. 'From the Flag, sir. *British Racer unable to steam or steer and has stopped engines. Suspected torpedo jammed between propellers and rudder. Investigation will be made*' The leading signalman looked up. 'Message ends, sir.'

Fanshawe stood there looking incredulous while his imagination got to work. Cameron glanced at Harcourt's face. The mid was deathly pale and no wonder. *British Racer* had to be on a knife-edge now; and there was probably nothing anybody could do about it. Just one slip could mean the end; and it was a chance in a million that the slow-moving torpedo had got itself stuck between the then revolving blades of the screws and hadn't gone up. The shafts must have come to a very sudden, very grinding stop that was unlikely to have done the engine-room any good. The fish might go up at any moment; even the automatic valves wouldn't prevent that unless the firing-pin could be withdrawn, and while it was jammed it wouldn't sink.

Fanshawe broke the silence. 'Now what?' he asked rhetorically. 'Do they abandon—just leave her to float about and eventually be sunk? Do we take the men off and sink her ourselves rather than let the Italians get the aviation spirit?' For the moment there was no answer to that. No doubt orders would come when more was known about the situation aboard the tanker. Cameron reported Rear-Admiral(D) altering towards the *British Racer*. The flotilla leader made up alongside and spoke to Captain Harcourt on the tanker's bridge, using his loud-hailer. Leaving the tanker's side, the Rear-Admiral passed close to *Burnside* and used his loudhailer again to speak to Fanshawe.

'Torpedo confirmed,' came the Rear-Admiral's voice. 'If it wasn't so bloody serious there'd be an element of comedy. It's got to be an Italian and not a German who fired at the extreme limit of range! The one that's wedged in *British Racer* must have been set lower in the water to end up where it did. The Master reports no trail observed.'

Fanshawe called back, 'Can it be freed, sir? Or the firing-pin be removed?'

'Not a hope without divers. If it wasn't for the fact that she's carrying a full cargo, all tanks filled, she might have trimmed down by the head to lift the stern. But that's out.'

'Then she might go at any minute, sir?'

'Well, not unless something triggers off that tin fish. It's tricky, very tricky, but it's not hopeless.'

'A tow, sir?'

'Yes. You, *Burgoyne* and *Brahmin*. You to stand by to give cover, the other two to pass a tow. All right, Fanshawe?'

'Yes, sir.'

'I'll be relying on you, so will the Admiral, to get her through the Gap and into Malta. The best of luck to you all . . . I shall ask Vice-Admiral Malta for an ocean-going rescue tug and divers.'

The flotilla leader moved ahead fast to pass the orders to *Burgoyne* and *Brahmin*. Closing them, he pulled up short with his engines moving full astern, acting like the brakes of a car. Away to starboard the attack was developing on the submarine: she wasn't going to get away with it. Fanshawe stared after the Rear-Admiral, his face set into deep lines. So much had not been said but the inference was obvious: as of now, they were on their own. The main part of the convoy and its escort could not afford to be held back by one lame duck, however valuable.

*　　　*　　　*

Nelson and *Rodney* were not to accompany the convoy through the Narrows: during the afternoon watch, by which time the enemy submarine had been destroyed by depth charge attack, the great battleships hauled off to the northeast with their destroyer screen, placing themselves protectively between the convoy and the Italian fleet bases. Cameron watched them go, conscious of a very naked feeling as the great steel walls drew away. By now the convoy with its cruisers and destroyers was hull-down to the east; *Burgoyne* and *Brahmin* had passed the tow, one on either bow of the tanker, and were proceeding east behind the convoy at four knots, with *Burnside* bringing up the rear and ready to deploy towards wherever danger might appear.

Fanshawe, still on the bridge, had spoken by loud-hailer to Captain Harcourt. 'Just to make things clear, Captain,' he'd said. 'I'm now the senior officer of your escort. I'd be obliged if you'd keep me closely informed.'

Harcourt waved in acknowledgement. 'You may be sure I'll do that!'

'I take it you'll keep all hands on deck throughout?'

'Yes. All except my Chief Engineer and an electrician who'll maintain a watch in the engine-room. Even though steam's shut off, there'll be a need for a watch—you'll understand that.'

'Quite.' Fanshawe paused. 'If it comes to a decision to abandon—'

'It won't,' Harcourt interrupted crisply. 'I've

no intention of abandoning. If I wanted to do that, now's the time. That torpedo's jammed fast—I've had a man down on a line, he saw it plain in this clear water. It's unlikely to shift in my opinion, but if it does decide to go up, well, it won't be giving us any warning.'

'I take your point,' Fanshawe called back. It was in all truth a case of now or never. It was going to be a very dicey operation; if the *British Racer* went up, so probably would *Burgoyne* and *Brahmin*. *Burnside* would possibly have a better chance, but not much better; it was Fanshawe's duty to remain close unless and until he had to move away to attack any intruder. By this time there was an uneasy atmosphere throughout the ship; no man could be in any doubt as to the immensity of the danger. It was all very well for the tanker's master to be so confident that the torpedo wouldn't shift. It might be shifted and blown by enemy action, it might shift if the weather worsened. According to Petty Officer Trent, torpedo-gunner's mate, the actual danger of the thing going up would depend just how it shifted. If it shifted nose down, all might be well; but if the warhead was brought into contact, with any degree of suddenness, with the tanker's side or with the screws or rudder-post, then that was that. It wouldn't take a big bang to detonate the fulminate of mercury in the nose.

Fanshawe asked, 'How the devil did it fetch

up where it did without exploding, then?'

Trent shrugged. 'Dunno, sir, that I don't. Magic, if you ask me! A miracle.'

'No theories?'

'Theories, yessir. Just sort of coasted in, like. Right slap on the end of its run, no punch left. I never 'eard the like before, sir. Don't suppose I ever will again.'

'It could be a dud, I suppose?'

'Yes, could be, sir, but I reckon that's too much like luck. None o' the others was duds, sir.'

Fanshawe nodded; in the event, the other torpedoes had not sunk as they should have done. Clearly, they had had their automatic valves adjusted so as to keep them afloat to be a menace to shipping: the submarine commander had decided to flout International Law and disregard the Convention—after all, it was mainly British convoys that passed this way. Trent had recalled that in the last war even British submarine skippers had carried out valve adjustments to keep their missed fish afloat, but only so a swimmer could be sent away to get up alongside the torpedo and remove the firing pin so that the fish could be recovered and used again. Anyway, on this occasion two destroyers had gone in to sink the torpedoes by gunfire as the convoy moved on eastwards. One by one they had all been accounted for; the resulting explosions had been proof enough that the fish had not been

116

duds.

However, when the torpedo-gunner's mate went below again, he dropped the word that the jammed fish *might* be a dud. Everyone liked to have hope to snatch at and—official words to the skipper apart—Trent saw no reason why he shouldn't give it to them whatever his own beliefs. Trent liked to spread happiness when possible. His own life was a model of happiness, or would be if it wasn't for Hitler and his war. Proof of that was fixed in photographic form on the deckhead in the PO's mess, just above where Trent slung his hammock, where he could gaze at it nightly before dropping off: Jessie, his wife. Some might have said she looked like a cottage loaf and some might have been right, but every roll of flesh was happy and good-natured. Jessie had been born and bred to the Navy; daughter of a man who'd made it to warrant rank and then lieutenant. Lieutenant Tubbs, who'd been CPO Tubbs when Trent was qualifying as an LTO at *Vernon*, the torpedo and anti-submarine school in Pompey. A good sort, well named—like his daughter he was fat. It had been love at first sight when Trent had met Jessie at a dance in *Vernon*. Now they had three fat children, all girls as it happened and the spit image of their mother. Trent, going aft to cast an eye over his torpedo-tubes, thought about the small rented house just off Highland Road in Southsea, not far from the cemetery.

117

Jessie used to like to sit in the cemetery while the kids played round the gravestones, it was quite an oasis, peaceful and green in summer. Sometimes, for a change and a day out, they used to take the ferry from the Hard across the harbour to Gosport and walk through to the naval cemetery at Haslar. Here were buried hundreds and hundreds of officers and ratings who had died on service ashore, many of them, from the days when disease was rife, pathetically young. It formed a piece of naval history, with many of the old-style ranks and ratings on the headstones: Fleet Surgeon, Assistant Clerk, sailmaker, captain of the foretop, lamptrimmer, gunroom cook's assistant, carpenter's mate, yeoman of stores, seaman pensioner. Just before the war had broken out Jessie had found what she reckoned was an ancestor: Elias Tubbs, able seaman in the dockyard hulks now replaced by the Royal Naval Barracks. It had made her day.

'Penny for 'em, Trent.' This was Mr Bartram, into whom Trent had all but bumped. Trent remembered the gunner's injury: mustn't knock him on his arse.

'Sorry, sir. Thoughts, eh? I was thinking of cemeteries as a matter of fact,' PO Trent said cheerfully.

'Don't. It's morbid.' Bartram paused. 'What d'you make the chances?'

'Fifty-fifty.'

Bartram nodded. 'Same here. But the odds'll shift like the fish itself if we get any near misses. Christ knows why the buggers are hanging back. Unless they're just waiting to get us in the Gap—which is more than likely.' He shaded his eyes with a hand and looked ahead across the placid blue water, towards the slow-moving tanker and the towing destroyers. The tow was steady, its central portion in each case keeping below the waterline as it should: trouble came when tows lifted clear of the sea. 'Much too bloody slow for comfort! Sitting ducks, that's us. Know what I'm going to do when the sods come in again?'

'Jump overboard and swim clear?'

Bartram chuckled. 'Got it in one. Take me own personal Carley float and pea-shooter. That apart, I'm going to bloody pray. There's bugger all else'll help us.'

Which sent Trent's mind back, via cemeteries—God's acres—to Jessie and the children. They'd been all right so far, got through the blitzes on Pompey. Barracks, Queen Street, King's Road, Palmerston Road, all the little streets south of the Guildhall, North End . . . so much that had been familiar and now would never be seen again. You couldn't recognize the place any more.

*   *   *

York's face was crumpled and vicious. He was

119

almost in tears. He'd gone into the galley flat and found Dewhurst's suitcase, tight shut and covered with a roll of coconut matting that had no business being there. In a frenzy he'd opened up and found Beano alive but in a nervous state. Three of the kittens were dead as mutton, suffocated by their mother and brothers and sisters as much as by the airless suitcase. York swore for five minutes flat, threatening vengeance against whoever was responsible. Beano clung to his body with sharp claws, mewing, her face reaching for his and ears flat aback. Cats always had wide eyes, but Beano's were really on the stretch and no wonder.

York went on swearing. He went out to the upper deck, plus Beano. Poor bloody cat, she needed all the air she could get. York encountered the gunner's mate, smart as ever, even shaved though the jowls were still dark.

'Watch the language,' Garter said.

'Bollocks. I don't see no women around.'

'And don't bloody answer back, you should know better than that. What's the trouble, eh?'

York began to explain in some detail but was cut short. 'Fuck the cat,' the gunner's mate said for the second time within an hour or two. 'Turn your mind towards the ship, all right?' He went off aft.

'And fuck you too,' York said bitterly, but kept it low.

*   *   *

They would not now make the Narrows before
first light next day; that would vastly increase
the dangers. Fanshawe cursed the existence of
the deep minefield. It had manufactured a
lethal bottleneck for anyone moving from east
to west or west to east through the
Mediterranean. As Senior Officer of the
group, he had to make decisions. He consulted
Cameron and the navigator, Mackenzie.

He said, 'We might do better to wait off the
entry. Wait for the next dark.'

'All day, sir?' Cameron asked.

'That's obvious from what I said, Cameron.'
There was an edge to the Captain's voice: he
was becoming a bag of nerves. 'It could be a
lesser risk. What d'you think, Pilot?'

'I doubt the lesser part, sir. We'd be wide
open to attack. Can't we increase the speed of
the tow?'

'That carries a risk, too. We can't risk
parting anything.'

Mackenzie said, 'I believe we could make
another two knots in this weather so long as it
holds. That wouldn't be enough, of course, but
at least we'd make some of the passage during
the dark hours.'

Fanshawe blew out his cheeks. 'I don't
know. The tanker's very deeply laden and she's
unhandy—very heavy. If she starts to yaw,
there's a real risk of parting the tow. But I

121

suppose we could try it.' He turned away and paced the bridge for a while. As always, it was a case of the right balance, one risk against another. Which was the greater? Fanshawe stopped and looked at the sea and the sky. The weather, the surface made currently as near perfect towing conditions as they were ever likely to get. Maybe this was the lesser risk. He made up his mind and faced his officers.

'Very well,' he said. 'We'll see what extra speed can be made in safety. Yeoman, make to all ships in company: *Speed of tow is to be increased to six knots. You are to watch the towing pendants carefully and reduce together instantly if either one lifts clear.*' He turned to Cameron. 'Just in case of trouble, Number One, we'll prepare to tow aft ourselves, all ready to pass a fresh pendant if it becomes necessary.'

'Aye, aye, sir.' Cameron left the bridge as the boatswain's mate started piping round the ship for the hands to muster aft. On the bridge there was renewed vigilance. The guns' crews would need immediate warning to return to their stations if the enemy should come in again.

*   *   *

Midshipman Harcourt was sent with Cameron, to assist and to gain experience. Preparing a tow was a complex business and could be a slow one. If it took place in bad weather conditions cable might have to be brought up from the cable-locker and ranged aft along the decks with the end passed through the after fairleads for shackling on to the towed vessel's pendant; but today it would be enough to prepare a heavy wire hawser with a coir or manila rope spring in the centre to give elasticity. Harcourt's mind was in something of a spin as he followed Cameron aft. He knew that he was the centre of massive interest: how must it feel, the eyes and expressions said, to have one's old man close by with a torpedo up his jacksie? Harcourt sensed sympathy along with the morbid interest, but he didn't want either. He just wanted to get on with the job and to be left alone otherwise. But he didn't mind Mr Bartram's friendly hand on his shoulder. Guns was a fatherly sort and not far off his father's age come to that, a father himself with a son on the lower deck, currently serving in a cruiser on the hated Murmansk run. Bartram said, 'Feeling the strain, course you are. Natural. So'll your dad be but he won't let it get him down. We can best help by looking on the bright side. If that fish was going to go up, why, it'd have gone up by now, stands to reason.'

'Does it?'

'Course it does! It's jammed as solid as—as a toad in a hole. If it shifts, well, I'll be the most bloody surprised gunner since that bloke

123

in the poem.'

'What poem?'

Mr Bartram scratched his head. 'Well, I'm not all that bloody precise on poetry, son, but it was about a British skipper that was outgunned and decided to scuttle like. "Sink me the ship, Master Gunner, sink her, split her in twain, for I'd sooner fall into the hands of God than fall into the hands of Spain." Words to that effect, anyway. Now—let's just get on with this lot, shall we?'

They did; the towing pendant was brought up on deck and ranged aft, its inboard end secured around the bitts, the outboard end ready by the fairlead. The main work would come later if the new tow had to be passed and *Burnside's* hawser made fast aboard the tanker. The hands were sent back to the guns and other stations; Cameron went to the bridge to report to the Captain. As he got there the W/T office was passing a weather report picked up on the routine broadcast to ships at sea. There was bad weather coming in the eastern Mediterranean, the glass was falling and a Levanter was starting to blow. Cameron knew what that portended: restless grey seas, overcast skies—not the weather for an easy tow. A Levanter might offer some protection against the attentions of the Stukas and the E boats to be expected in the Gap, but in all other respects it would be a dead loss. The Mediterranean could be as vicious weatherwise as the North Atlantic when it really made up its mind to it.

Fanshawe said, 'If it strikes us, we reduce the speed of the tow immediately. I don't need to underline the dangers.'

He didn't. The torpedo, however solidly jammed, could shift in a seaway.

*   *   *

The weather remained fair until 1700 hours when there were visible indications of a coming change. The barometric pressure was tending downwards and there was a slight but noticeable fall in temperature; also a different look in the sky. The blue had turned a greenish metallic colour and there was some cloud scudding over from easterly. In the meantime the tow was taking the extra speed well enough; the towing pendants were keeping below the surface and there was only a very slight yaw on the tanker, hard as it was for the destroyers to hold her steady without some assistance from her rudder, now from force of circumstances as motionless as her propellors. Captain Harcourt was watching the tow as carefully as the men on the destroyers' bridges even though he would be totally powerless to rectify matters if anything should part. He was finding it a highly frustrating business. No master welcomed being at the mercy of another ship even at the best of times. He tried

125

without any success whatsoever not to think about the high explosive tied to his tail. He had not had the benefit of having heard Bartram's optimism about the torpedo remaining static; if he had, he wouldn't have put too much faith in it and never mind what he had called across to the destroyer earlier. Jammed it certainly was, but apparently-well-jammed objects could be funny things and didn't always behave as expected. One aspect above all was worrying Captain Harcourt: he had lives to consider. They were, in his view, more important than his cargo. Whatever his aversion to abandoning, the option to do so did exist. He mustn't forget that. On the other hand, the arrival of his cargo in Malta could save other lives, many more lives, by adding to the island's defence capability. That had to be taken into account as well, and was no doubt the overriding consideration in the minds of the Admiral, now departed aboard the *Nelson*, and of the senior officer of the tanker's personal escort close by in *Burnside*.

Nevertheless, only one man could make the decision to order the abandoning of the *British Racer* and that was himself, Captain Hamilton Harcourt, Master Mariner—Master, in the words of the traditional seafaring formula, under God. God would be the final judge, as in all matters. Harcourt debated within his mind as he paced his wide bridge and looked down at his tank-tops. He could send some of his

126

men over to the escort, where they would have a better chance; but he could spare few of his deck complement with the ship under tow. They had to be there in an emergency, maybe to take another tow. As for his officers, the same applied—and none of them would be keen to leave while the fo'c'sle hands were kept aboard. The engine-room? Perhaps a few could be spared, but again there was the question of emergencies that could arise even when steam was shut down. And there was another factor that had to be borne in mind: further attack was bound to come and a near miss could, just could with a lot of luck, shake that torpedo safely clear so that he could steam. It would be suicide to hang about during an attack while he got his men back from the escort. He had to have enough to put steam on the main engines and set a watch in the engine-room and boiler-room. One of the differences between a merchant ship and a naval ship, a warship, was that the latter was always manned on the basis of an action complement, which meant one hell of a lot of spare hands around when the ship wasn't in action—guns' crews, torpedo crews, back-up hands, magazine and shell-handling parties and so on. Merchant ships were manned on a pared-down working basis, which meant that every man counted. Counted all the time. Not that he couldn't spare a few nevertheless.

Harcourt was about to hail the *Burnside* to

take off some of his men when the next attack, so long delayed, came in.

CHAPTER NINE

'Aircraft bearing red 135, sir!'

Fanshawe swung round. 'Sound action stations.' Once again the savage note of the alarm rattlers tore through the ship. There were black specks coming straight out of the lowering sun, black specks high in the sky that turned quickly into diving, angry bees. The Stukas again; plus what looked like a whole squadron of torpedo-bombers.

'Quarters firing . . . each gun fire when the sights come on.' Fanshawe felt the run of sweat down his face. Each gun . . . damn it, effectively he had only the twin HA mounting plus the close-range stuff, the multiple pom-poms, the Oerlikons and some small machine-guns in the bridge wings. In aerial attack, the main surface armament might just as well not exist, though a dead lucky shell aimed at a low-level torpedo-bomber and hitting it was always a possibility. 'It's up to us now, Number One. *Burgoyne* and *Brahmin* are virtually in irons.'

Cameron nodded. The tow was very restricting to say the least. *Burnside* could manoeuvre freely, and did so. She turned this way and that as the bombs screamed down, all her ack-ack weapons firing continuously. The other two destroyers were adding to the racket and the myriad puffs of smoke that broke as the shrapnel burst above them. Early on, two of the Stukas were hit and plummeted down into the sea, trailing smoke, their wings breaking off on impact. The sharp stench of gunsmoke filled the air. Beneath the bursting shells the tow proceeded at its six knots while *Burnside* circled the three ships, as protective as possible. Below in the engine-room the Commissioned Engineer watched the sprung bulk-head carefully, his face anxious: every time the skipper went into his twist-and-turn antics extra strain came on and the seepage worsened a little. The plates came together again as the ship straightened but each time water came in. There was quite a slop. It was worse on the turn to port, since that brought the sea farther up the starboard side as she heeled to full wheel: centrifugal bloody force, Canton reflected, cursing its existence as a fact of life. He ducked as a rivet went and spun dangerously across the starting platform.

He called the bridge.

'Engine-room, sir. Rivet just gone.'

'Can you cope, Chief? Do you want some hands from the damage control parties?'

Canton said, 'No, we'll manage.'

'Keep me informed.'

'Aye, aye, sir.' Mr Canton grabbed for a hand-hold as the destroyer swung again. He could imagine what it must be like up top and he didn't see any way they could come through. Any minute now; if that poor bloody tanker went it could take them all with it. Just as he thought that there was an almighty explosion close by to port. Everything danced and shook in the engine-room. The lights went out, then came on again almost immediately. Mr Canton said, 'Jesus Christ on Clarence Pier,' and slid on his bottom off the starting platform as the ship lurched heavily.

On the upper deck the gunner's mate had also slid, knocked off his feet to fetch up against Number Four gun mounting aft. He picked himself up, shook a furious but useless fist at the Stuka now climbing out of its dive. It had been a close thing; there could be damage below. Cameron came aft at the rush, accompanied by the buffer and a shipwright, and went in through the after screen. The gunner's mate felt a nasty twinge in his back. Not a wound, just age—he was getting too old to be chucked about like a doll. No use making a fuss about it, but he had difficulty in walking, let alone moving at the double. As fast as he could he climbed the ladder to the shelter deck. That Stuka had used its machine-guns as it dived, used them, so far as Garter could see, against the searchlight platform on the midships super-structure and the pom-poms alongside it. There could be trouble.

There was: the pom-poms were manned by

130

the dead and dying, and one of the Oerlikons had an inert body swinging in the straps. The gunner's mate moved painfully aft and shouted down to Number Four mounting.

'You there, Leading Seaman Dewhurst. Leave that bloody useless article, bring your guns' crews up here, sharpish. Come on, *move!*'

He went back to the close-range weapons, slithering on blood. Working fast, he got the body clear of the Oerlikon straps and got in himself, feeling murderous, his dark jowls moving in loud oaths. When the next lot came in he held his fire and let the bugger have it just at the right instant. He squeezed the trigger vengefully and saw the windscreen shatter and blood obliterate the pilot's face. Once again the bombing was close, but that one wouldn't be dropping any more. It smashed into the sea about a cable's-length off the port beam and that was that. Garter's face was devilish, but his mind was cold and working clearly. He swung his gun to meet the next attack. By this time Dewhurst was manning the pom-poms with his guns' crews from aft, revolving the platform, elevating the barrels. The barrage was tremendous, coming fast and furious from all three ships. The usual protective umbrella, but this time seeming miraculously heavy. They were out on their own, with no support, but what guns they had were putting everything into it. A little too

131

much, perhaps; too much enthusiasm, not enough care. The gunner's mate, easing his aching body in the straps of the Oerlikon, a momentary spell between bursts, glanced towards the port pom-pom and nearly froze: the multiple barrels had swung bang on to him.

He yelled, 'Dewhurst, for Christ's sake, *bloody elevate*!'

He sank in the straps just in time. Cannon shells sped over where his head had been. Some smacked off the pole mast carrying the HF/DF. The air around the gunner's mate was blue. Bloody Dewhurst, not fit to fry an egg. Dewhurst looked badly shaken. The mounting must have developed a defect: it seemed to have travelled beyond its safe bearing stops.

*   *   *

'Bomb loads evidently all dropped,' Fanshawe said, wiping his streaming face. The Stukas and the torpedo-bombers were climbing; the attack was over. It would come again, but for now the little flotilla was intact. That was Fanshawe's thought: one of sheer gratitude for a respite during which they would come closer to Malta. It had been a tense action of split-second timing to avoid the bombs and torpedoes, of attempting, with success as it happened, to deflect the enemy aircraft from their main target, the *British Racer*.

In point of fact it wasn't over yet. The

enemy aircraft hadn't all gone. Cameron, reporting to the bridge that all was shipshape below, saw the solitary torpedo-bomber, very low over the water to port, seeming to hover, camouflaged by the sea itself, like some malignant gnat. Cameron shouted, 'Attack port, sir!'

Fanshawe swung round in time to see the torpedo drop into the water. As soon as it was launched the aircraft started to gain height. Once more, all the guns opened. No use: the torpedo-bomber banked, turning away to head after the others, and made it safely out of range. From *Burnside*'s bridge the torpedo-trail couldn't yet be seen; but Fanshawe passed the orders to take his ship round the tanker's stern to come up on her port side. He was the escort, the only ship that could manoeuvre in protection of his charge, and the tanker had to be preserved at all costs.

Everyone knew that. Putting the helm over, Chief Petty Officer Dickens in the wheelhouse was phlegmatic about it, Fanshawe having passed down the facts. If *Burnside* was put across the track of that tin fish, whether or not Dickens saw Devonport again would depend on just whereabouts it hit. It could have his number on it; if so, that was that, nothing he could do about it except obey orders as they came down to him from the skipper. It was what he had joined for, what he had been trained for, what he had trained others for.

Dickens, as the destroyer swung, watched his gyro repeater and also watched the faces of his wheelhouse staff, his helmsman, a leading seaman ready to take over the wheel if he himself copped it, and two ordinary seamen who worked the engine-room telegraphs and acted as messengers. The leading hand was all right, smoking a fag unconcernedly and reclining on his arse, more or less comfortable on the deck. The ordinary seamen had the shakes, had had them all the way through. They were both hostilities-only ratings, hadn't wanted to go to war and according to the buffer made more than ordinarily cack-handed seamen. But they had guts; dead scared as they were, they'd borne up, carried on, obeyed orders. You couldn't ask for more than that, Dickens thought. It must be bloody hard, to be dragged off to war when it had never occurred to you to make a career of the Navy . . .

'Midships.'

'Midships, sir.' Dickens let the wheel spin back through his hands. 'Wheel's amidships, sir.'

'Steady.'

'Steady, sir. Course—' Dickens broke off. There had been a big explosion and the destroyer shuddered to it, but it hadn't been *Burnside* that had been hit. No more orders came down just yet and Dickens maintained the course he had been steering when the skipper had said steady. He wondered what was going on outside; in action the wheelhouse depended wholly on the voice-pipe and the sound-powered telephone. In action the deadlights were clamped down over the ports.

A moment later the Captain's voice came down again. '*Burgoyne*'s been hit for'ard and is going down.'

*   *   *

Up on the bridge Fanshawe was staring in disbelief: the end was coming very suddenly, astonishingly suddenly. The torpedo had ripped into the destroyer's innards. Normally she could have been expected to survive, but her for'ard magazines must have gone and ripped the bottom out of her, probably from the stem to the midship section. Men were doubling aft along her decks with an obvious intent: to cast off the tow.

'They'll never make it,' Fanshawe said. He looked away to starboard, towards the *British Racer*: there, too, men were running along the deck to the fo'c'sle-head. As *Burnside* moved in to take off survivors, the *Burgoyne*'s angle of dip increased sharply and the sea surged back over her bridge and superstructure. A moment later she was gone, leaving bobbing heads and a whirlpool of water where her stern had vanished. The heavy towing pendant came briefly clear of the water as the immense strain came on, then, bar taut, started to slant down

135

and move back towards the tanker's bows. Then it parted; the rope spring ensured that there was not much in the way of a lash-back. The towing pendant fell slack, straight up-and-down from the tanker's bows.

Fanshawe said, 'We'll have to take over, Number One. Tow aft, soonest possible.'

'The weather reports, sir—'

'Yes, I know. It's coming towards us already.' The sea was ruffled by what was as yet a light wind and the temperature had fallen a little more. 'We must prepare for a blow, Number One. Bad-weather procedure, using the cables.' Fanshawe added, 'Once we're shackled on, *Brahmin* will have to bring out cable as well.'

*   *   *

As in the case of the troopship, the survivors were all too few. Many men had been killed when the torpedo hit, and *Burgoyne* had suffered badly in the action already. Two guns' crews had been wiped out and there had been a large number of casualties from machine-gunning. In addition to all this, the desperate attempt to cast off the tow before any damage could be caused to the tanker had cost lives. The seamen had delayed too long, and many had been sucked under as the destroyer went down. Of those rescued some were picked up by *Brahmin*, others reached the tanker, more from necessity of nearness than from choice, and were brought aboard from jumping-ladders. Those of the survivors who were brought aboard *Burnside* uninjured were welcome enough as replacements for the men killed. The guns apart, the operation of getting up cable for the new tow was a job for all hands.

As the heavy links were brought up from the cable-locker and led along the decks towards the after fairleads under Cameron's orders Leading Seaman York detached himself briefly from the work in hand and went into the galley flat to take a look at Beano.

He found Dewhurst there.

'Bugger off,' he said.

'I'm seeing to the cat.'

'Leave the cat alone.'

'Why?'

'Because I say so, that's why.' York's face was belligerent. 'Cack-'anded twit, done enough damage, I reckon. I 'eard you bloody nearly shot the GI. Mind you, some say that's what they're there for. But it don't speak too well for *your* bloody abilities, *Mister* Dewhurst—'

'You're back on that again, are you?' Dewhurst's voice was high, betraying ragged nerves. 'If you like you can carry on, I don't care. Before the war you'd have called me that anyway, if not sir. So—'

'*Sir? You?* You little bleeder. Just because

you went to one o' them soft public schools, all I say what an' feel me chopper after tuck. Load of nancy boys and teachers to match. Up the school an' up a lot else as well.' York was right into his stride when the gunner's mate looked in, having heard the loud, angry voice. It didn't take him long to sum up the situation.

'Now then you two! Not the way for leading 'ands to carry on. Back on deck, York. Work to be done.'

'Look, this little—'

'That's an order, York. Smack it about, look sharp.'

York met the gunner's mate's eye and lumbered off. Garter surveyed Dewhurst, looking sardonic. He said, 'Kiss my arse. I don't know what we're expected to do about you. You have me flummoxed. Nearly killed me, nearly swept the bridge clean. If the director hadn't been out of action, you'd have done for the lot of 'em up there.'

'I'm sorry, GI. It was the gun—'

'You could be sorrier soon. Just watch it. Apart from your own ratings on the gun, no one saw it but me. If you were about to say, which I reckon you were, that the pom-pom shouldn't have been able to come round to a dangerous bearing, I'll go along with that. It'll be looked at. But that's the sort of thing a leading 'and's there to check and cope with, right? Don't let it happen again, that's all, or you'll be for the 'igh jump, lad.' The gunner's

138

mate looked across at the open suitcase. 'This your mission in naval life, then?'

'I'm just helping out, that's all.'

'Go and help out on deck or I'll have you for skulking.' Garter turned about and marched away, smartly despite the pain in his back. Like all gunner's mates he seemed to be giving himself the step: left, right, left, shoulders back, stomach in, chest out, swing those arms. It was very difficult aboard a destroyer but Garter managed it all right. Dewhurst followed him out of the galley flat, looking and feeling a shambles by comparison. The upper deck seemed to be a sort of controlled bedlam, with sweating, cursing seamen heaving away at the cable, dragging it aft on short lengths of rope fed through the links. Paintwork was going for a burton as the heavy steel clanked and tumbled and banged past the bulkheads. By the time the cable-end was aft and led through the fairlead with the wire towing pendant secured the dusk was not far off and there was the beginning of a sea running beneath skies turned grey and threatening. They were going to be just about in time.

Cameron reported to the bridge: 'Tow ready to be passed, sir.'

'Right—thank you, Number One.' Fanshawe looked aft towards the tanker, then spoke to the leading signalman. 'Call up the *British Racer*. Tell him I'm ready. When he gives the word, I'll drop astern and take his heaving line.'

'Aye, aye, sir.'

Within the next five minutes Captain Harcourt's signal came that he was ready to take the tow. Fanshawe called down through a megaphone: 'Stand by aft.'

There was a wave from Cameron.

'Engines slow astern. Wheel ten degrees to starboard.' Once again Fanshawe looked towards the *British Racer* as his ship began to inch astern. The tanker's cable had been veered, her anchors hung off on heavy wire strops. She was steady in the water but *Burnside* was rolling a little now, just to make the job a little harder, a little more dangerous to life and limb. Heavy gear was being played around with. In the eyes of the *British Racer* stood the ship's boatswain, who would cast the heaving line himself. There was an art in casting heaving lines against a rising wind, and there was an art in catching them, too. As the destroyer slowly closed the gap, the heaving line was thrown, coming straight as a die, snaking across the darkening water behind the heavy monkey's-fist that gave it the necessary weight. Fanshawe heard the loudly shouted reaction as the monkey's-fist took Leading Seaman York unawares, full in the mouth.

'Soddin' thing.'

It was Cameron who caught the line before it slid back over the side. Hands grabbed it and

140

heaved in strongly until the eye of the grass messenger to which it was attached was brought aboard and taken to the drum of a winch. As soon as the turns were on, the winch was started and the tanker's cable began to move towards the destroyer's stern. When the shackle was brought aboard the towing pendant was secured, the messenger was cast off, and the tow was eased back into the water. Once again, when all was secure, Cameron reported to the bridge. Fanshawe signalled the *British Racer* that he had the tow and proposed to move ahead dead slow until the strain was taken, and after that he would increase gradually to a safe speed. In the meantime, *Brahmin* would cast off her fair-weather tow and prepare cable as in the case of *Burnside*.

The strain was taken up; *Brahmin* cast off as ordered. Until she re-shackled, the whole weight of the tow would come on *Burnside*'s cable-clench and the slips.

Together they moved into the gathering night and the increasing wind, heading for the Gap, the narrow pathway through the deep minefield, the lookouts straining their eyes to all points of the compass, watching for the re-emergence of the enemy.

CHAPTER TEN

Surgeon Lieutenant Fleming was suffering a strong sense of frustration as he watched men die. He was on his own with pathetically few resources as compared with a shoreside hospital. He had, it was true, the assistance of the LSBA from the *Burgoyne*, but only up to a point. The man was in a wretched state of nerves after the blowing up of his ship. He had told Fleming that *Burgoyne's* doctor had been blown up by the torpedo. A man, one of the damage control parties, had been injured by a fall down the ladder to the stokers' messdeck and the doctor had gone along to see to him and was there when the torpedo hit. No one had come out of that. Fleming had known *Burgoyne's* doctor and the news had shaken him. There was too much to do for him to dwell on it, but it was there at the back of his mind as he did what he could for broken limbs, torn stomachs, chests with steel splinters embedded in them. There were a number of emergency operations to be performed under virtually impossible conditions, with his own LSBA acting as anaesthetist. If anyone survived, Fleming thought, it would be a miracle. Though he was doing his best, of course, he was a physician, not a surgeon, and never mind his title of Surgeon Lieutenant.

There were not enough of them to go round to appoint a physician and a surgeon to every ship, and men had no option but to take their chance.

He was operating, making an attempt to remove a six-inch jag of grey-painted steel bulkhead from the region of the kidneys, something he had never had to do before, when the destroyer started its roll. He said, 'Call the bridge, Trott. Ask the Captain if he can steady the ship,'

The LSBA, recognizing that some things were beyond the control even of the Captain, nevertheless obeyed orders. He spoke to the Officer of the Watch, who expressed concern but said the doctor would have to manage as best he could.

Fleming gritted his teeth. One slip and the man on the wardroom table was going to die. War was a bastard. He concentrated on intricacies of cutting and probing, trying to recall all he had ever learned about kidneys. God help sailors on a night like this ... the cable clanked and banged along the deck above and the ship seemed to be juddering throughout her plates. Dust and fragments of cork insulation dropped around him from the deckhead: antisepsis, here afloat, was just something you read about in books. He probed away, sweating into his face mask.

The LSBA said, 'He's gone, sir.'

'What?'

'Gone. Dead. No use going on.'

'Oh, Christ. I'd better sew him up again.'

LSBA Trott gave him an odd look. 'Wouldn't bother with that, sir. There's others waiting. Next time he needs sewing it'll be into his hammock.'

Fleming straightened, easing his back. He thought, if only the ship had been steady, I might have saved him. He made ready for the next case, a man moaning on a high note and staring at him fixedly, the eyes terrified.

*   *   *

The tow was steadier once *Brahmin* was back with them, helping to take the weight; nevertheless, with the increasing wind and sea, the tanker was yawing badly and this was causing anxiety, throwing extra strain on the tow. It was a nightmare business of constant watchfulness, of constantly easing the engines and hoping that the order had been passed to the starting platform in time. After full dark Cameron had prevailed upon the Captain to get some sleep while he held the fort: Fanshawe would be called immediately if anything happened. He had refused at first, snappishly, but had agreed when he'd fallen into a dead sleep in his bridge chair and had rolled sideways, hitting his head as he fell.

Below in the engine-room Mr Canton remained on watch. He didn't trust anyone else to be quite as alert as himself and he wanted to watch the sprung plates, which had been getting a shade more troublesome as the weather deteriorated. Besides, he didn't really feel the lack of sleep. Funny, that; the older he got the less sleep he seemed to need. He was quite perky.

He clicked his tongue at the slop of seawater moving to and fro on the engine-room floor as the destroyer rolled. Bugger it. If that got much worse it wouldn't be funny, but there was nothing further he could do until they got the ship into dockyard hands. Mr Canton regarded that prospect with mixed feelings: he didn't like dockyards nor the dockyard mateys who worked in them; nor the little pompous fussy men in bowler hats who controlled the dockyard mateys and had the bloody cheek to take over his engine-room once the ship was in their hands. Not long ago he'd had a fracas in the Clyde; one of the civilian shipyards, not on that occasion a royal dockyard, but they were just as bad. Some machinery had got to be taken out and it had involved the removal of a ladder leading up to a hatch, a very simple job, but the shipyard gang hadn't come prepared for it. Mr Canton had said he would see to that, get some hands on it right away, but they'd said oh, no, no. Removal of ladders, that was very strictly for one of their trade union brothers, a demarcation thing. Not to be touched by the ship's crew, or by themselves.

Bollocks, Mr Canton had said.

It might be bollocks to the Navy, their spokesman had retorted, but to them it was not bollocks. It was solidarity. If Mr Canton's men touched that ladder, a strike would be called and the whole Clyde would come out.

In the middle of a war! Mr Canton had been speechless but had been defeated. He and his Chief ERA had been forced to hang around while a properly qualified ladder remover had been found and had agreed to operate—by this time at overtime rates chalked up to the Admiralty—and in the upshot the ship had been delayed sailing to join a convoy for eight hours.

It made you bloody puke.

The Clyde seemed a long, long way off now and the farther the better for Mr Canton. He'd have liked to have had some of those demarcation-minded bastards out here in the Med and see if they quoted bulkhead proppers-up at him if those plates started to go in earnest. He'd have battened them down with the rising waters and told them it wasn't his job to open up, they'd best wait for one of the brethren.

As he was pondering on all this, the action alarm went. He blew out his cheeks and mopped at his face with his bunch of cotton-waste. He needn't have worried about going into dockyard hands; three ships joined together at dead slow speed would never have a cat in hell's chance of getting through.

*   *   *

It had been Midshipman Harcourt, at his gun station, who had spotted them first: the E boats, nasty little fast craft, almost certainly Italian out here, carrying torpedoes and presenting only small targets. The bridge had been informed and Fanshawe had been called. The guns were quickly in action from *Burnside* and *Brahmin*, a murderous protective barrage that ripped into the night. Almost immediate success was gained: distantly there was an explosion that for a brief while lit the area like day. One of the E boats had blown up together with her load of torpedoes. Soon after this another went: the E boats had been unlucky, they preferred to remain unseen until they had made their approach and sent off their fish, after which they would scarper. A moment later Cameron saw an approaching trail quite clearly. He held his breath. The torpedo passed harmlessly but nerve-tearingly between *Burnside's* stern and the bows of the *British Racer*. One gone, so many more to go.

Fanshawe said, 'No damn manoeuvrability, Number One!'

'Slip the tow, sir?'

'What?' Fanshawe hesitated; sleep or the lack of it had invaded his mind. He came to a

147

decision. 'Yes, I think you're right. Fast as you can.'

Cameron was down the ladder in a flash, shouting above the sound of the guns. The hands assembled aft; with no time lost a blacksmith's hammer knocked away the pin of the joining shackle left on deck. The destroyer gave a bottom-waggle as the towing pendant and the tanker's cable jerked away in the water astern and the weight came off. At once Fanshawe increased speed and put the helm over, leaving the tow in the care of *Brahmin*. *Burnside* leaped away, hard-a-port towards the E boats, moving fast and throwing up a big bow wave as the screws bit. The Italians scattered, firing back with their close range weapons, their torpedo attack thrown off. *Burnside's* 4.7-inch armament and the Oerlikons kept up a constant fire; two more of the torpedo-boats were caught and blew up. The rest had had enough. They withdrew at high speed, having inflicted no damage. The sound of their engines died away into the night.

Fanshawe said, 'Well, we've learned a lesson. I'll not reconnect the tow. It's better to be free to fight back even if we're that much slower and the tanker harder to handle. Right, Number One?'

'Yes, sir. Shall I restow the cable?'

Fanshawe shook his head. 'No. Leave it ready. *Brahmin* could get hit.' He looked

148

round as the leading signalman came up. 'Yes?'

'From *British Racer*, sir. Torpedo believed shifted.'

*   *   *

On board the tanker the atmosphere was more tense than ever. There had been a clang aft, a clang of short duration but one that had echoed throughout the ship below, very noticeable in the engine-room where the Chief Engineer was still keeping his vigil. The engine-room was right aft, very close to the jammed torpedo. In fact, almost above it. The noise had been highly alarming and the Chief Engineer felt some surprise that he was still there and alive to report it to the bridge.

Captain Harcourt had heard it too. Since it had come right on the heels of the jettisoning of *Burnside's* share of the tow, Harcourt saw a connection. As the cable had been freed aboard the destroyer the towing pendant and the tanker's cable on its other end had plunged down into the sea and there had been a decided jerk on his bows.

That could just have been enough to shift the torpedo. Harcourt's reaction had been harsh. The Navy were all very well but their guns came first—no doubt they had to, he admitted that, and the destroyer had dealt firmly with the E boats all said and done—but in Harcourt's view Fanshawe should have thought about that torpedo and the likely consequences of a sudden jerk. If Harcourt had been aboard the destroyer, he would have gone astern first, backing up and giving the tanker a chance to heave in on her cable so that the weight would have been less when the pin was knocked out aboard *Burnside*.

Now he had to take the result of haste.

He went aft accompanied by a man with a yardarm group, a cluster of lights on the end of a trailing lead. This was lowered to the waterline and Harcourt, on the end of another line, went over the side to look for himself.

He couldn't see much if anything; the light just reflected back off the water. He called up for the line to be paid out. He went deep, fighting his way down with difficulty. Using a powerful battery torch, the sort used to look down to the distant bottoms of empty tanks, protected against the making of sparks by its heavy rubber insulation, he peered about. The water was clear enough. The beam picked up the torpedo and Harcourt saw the nose, the thin metal that covered the fulminate of mercury that would detonate it. His lungs at bursting point he jerked on the line and was hauled up to the surface and brought aboard, assisted over the bulwarks by his Chief Officer.

'You all right, sir?'

'I'm all right. I can't speak for that bloody torpedo.' Harcourt dripped water and breathed heavily. 'It's shifted, I believe—it's not lying quite as it was reported to me, though the refraction of the water could have given it a different appearance on the first inspection, I suppose.'

'Any chance of getting a line round it now, sir?'

Harcourt shook his head. 'Much too risky.'

'Is there a worse lie now?'

Harcourt gave a bitter laugh. 'Couldn't be much worse. The nose is aimed straight for the hull. I'll have a word with the RN for what it's worth.'

*   *   *

There was, as Harcourt had known, nothing to be done about it but to move on and hope for the best. The tow proceeded through the moonless dark, through the rising wind from the east. Fanshawe had raised the obvious question at the start: could the torpedo's warhead be rendered safe? The answer was that in theory the firing-pin could be removed but the risk would be enormous in the absence of properly equipped and experienced divers. It was not the kind of job that could be attempted by men who would need to keep coming to the surface for air. The risk would be greater than if they just kept plodding on. Now, with the worsening weather, it had become impossible.

151

There was no relaxation throughout the destroyer: everything was on a knife-edge; when the explosion came there would be no warning. But there was a determination to get the *British Racer* through to Malta and give the lie to Mussolini's boast of *mare nostrum*. The Med was still British and was going to remain so. Cameron met the feeling wherever in the ship he went. There was no despondency. Leading Seaman York put it into words. He said, 'Musso can go an' get stuffed, sir. We was 'ere when 'e was no more'n a twinkle in 'is dad's eye.'

PO Garter made his rounds of the guns, grim-faced and more formidable than ever. He wasn't going to be chased out of the Med either. He made his point by picking more holes than he'd ever picked before, checking, rasping at the guns' crews, checking again. They had to be on top line, just like at the gunnery school ashore. No slackness permitted. The guns were all they had, the whole reason for their existence, and nothing else mattered. At each gun Garter left muttered curses behind him: he was a right bastard, was the GI. There was disagreement on that point, but only in a technical direction. Garter, according to Leading Seaman York, couldn't be a bastard. Why? Well, gunner's mates weren't born at all in the ordinary sense; they were quarried.

Midshipman Harcourt, at his station as

152

officer of the quarters aft, was filled with fear for the *British Racer*. The odds were heavily against his father's survival now. He would not have grieved less had news come from, say, the Indian Ocean or the South Atlantic that his father had been lost; but this was going to be much more immediate. His sheer helplessness tore at him. He thought also about his mother; how would she take it? That was an imponderable; Harcourt was remembering those past liaisons in his father's absences at sea. But she was getting older now and would miss him, miss the security at any rate. Cameron, checking round the ship like the gunner's mate, saw the midshipman staring towards the tanker. He hesitated a moment, then moved on. There was nothing he could say that would help. Better to be absolutely normal; sympathy, at this stage, would be misplaced.

Cameron moved for'ard and climbed to the bridge. Fanshawe was still sitting in his chair, a dark shadow bracing himself against the bridge screen. He looked round as Cameron came up.

'Is that you, Number One?'

'Yes, sir. All correct, sir.'

'I've had a report from the engine-room. The water's coming in more.'

'Yes, I know. I've just been down there. Mr Canton's coping, sir.'

'Let's hope he can cope for long enough.' Fanshawe turned in his seat. 'Pilot, how long now to the Narrows?'

Mackenzie sighed; this was perhaps the fiftieth time the Captain had asked that question. He said, 'Three hours, sir.' Fanshawe nodded. In a few moments he would be asking again, Mackenzie thought. It was as though he was losing his grip, getting old before his time, unable to keep things in his mind. *Burnside* was circling the other two ships now, acting not as a sheepdog but a guard. Continual alterations of course were going down to the wheelhouse, where CPO Dickens was taking a spell from the wheel, which he'd handed over to Leading Seaman Willett. Willett fancied the officers on the bridge must be getting giddy, round and round like a spinning-top. He lit a Players and inhaled deeply. When he exhaled the smoke went up the voice-pipe. Officers were unlucky; they couldn't smoke on the bridge during the dark hours and his exhaled smoky breath might come as a benison, or just might make them envious for once of the lower deck. On the floor, with his back against the bulkhead, the coxswain began snoring. Willett lifted his eyes to heaven. As if it wasn't bad enough, moving in circles round imminent castastrophe. Willett wondered how the rest of the convoy had been faring, the ones who had peeled off and gone ahead; with luck, they might be through the Gap and beginning their approach to Malta. With another sort of luck, the poor bastards might be drawing off the

Eyeties from the *British Racer* and her escorts. The Eyeties might not bother any more with just one merchant ship, however valuable. That was a comforting thought but it wasn't due to last longer than the expiring night: the bridge had just passed the word down, informatively, that dawn was coming up when the ship went once again to panic stations.

*   *   *

It wasn't much: just one Italian aircraft coming in from the north-west. 'Sardinia, probably,' Fanshawe said. 'She won't attack, just report back to base.'

Cameron, looking through his binoculars, said a few seconds later, 'I think she's on an attack course, sir.'

'Bugger!' Fanshawe lifted his glasses again. 'Can you identify yet?'

'Torpedo-bomber, sir.'

'We'll keep her at bay,' Fanshawe said. 'All guns, fire when ready.'

Within a minute the barrage started. The torpedo-bomber came on regardless. To the personnel on the destroyer's bridge it looked like suicide. On the other hand the aircraft was keeping low, little more than a couple of feet clear of the surface, largely beneath the angle of depression of the guns. Two torpedoes were seen to drop from beneath the belly; still the aircraft kept low, still on course towards the three ships. The port lookout reported the torpedo trails, not easily identified in the confused sea. One of them appeared to be heading straight for the *British Racer*. The other would probably pass astern. In the event, both of them missed. But before that was known the torpedo-bomber had lifted into the air to pass over the three ships. By now the gunfire was intense; it seemed utterly impossible that any aircraft could live through it, unless she gained height fast which the Italian was now too late to do. As she approached her cannons opened, spraying the tanker's bridge, cutting through the wheelhouse, and then she turned to attack both the destroyers in a similar way.

On *Burnside's* bridge Mackenzie fell dead across the gyro repeater and the voice-pipe; Fanshawe staggered back against the screen with his right forearm streaming blood. Moments after passing over *Brahmin* the aircraft burst into flames, then exploded, scattering metal fragments. Looking across towards *Brahmin*, Cameron fancied that a clean sweep had been made of her bridge. And something similar appeared to have happened aboard the tanker.

CHAPTER ELEVEN

There was a man waving from the *British Racer*'s bridge—waving and shouting through a megaphone. His words couldn't be heard. Fanshawe said, 'Close her, Number One.'

'Are you all right, sir?'

'Yes. I said, close her.'

'Aye, aye, sir.' Cameron eased Mackenzie's body aside and passed the orders, sending at the same time for the Surgeon Lieutenant. The destroyer came up close to the tanker's port side. Fanshawe had his loud hailer switched on.

'What's the damage?' he called across.

'Captain's badly wounded. All other deck officers killed, and a number of deckhands too.'

'And you?'

'Gutteridge, sir, boatswain.'

'Can you cope?'

'I reckon so, yes.'

Fanshawe said, 'I'll send my doctor to see to the Master.'

'Right you are, sir. I'll rig a jumping ladder.'

'Yes, do that. Port side.' Fanshawe switched off the loud hailer. As he did so, Fleming came up the ladder. He had his LSBA with him, plus bandages. He examined the Captain's arm. The cannon shell had given a glancing hit.

Fanshaw had been lucky; it could have exploded. As it was, it had just taken a chunk of flesh with it. Fleming said there was nothing that wouldn't heal. Fanshawe nodded his thanks and turned to the leading signalman, who was waiting with a report. The Captain lifted an eyebrow.

'From *Brahmin*, sir. Captain dead, two officers seriously wounded. First Lieutenant assumed command.'

Fanshawe nodded sombrely. 'I'm sorry.' Then he turned to Cameron. 'The tanker, Number One. No officers. No doubt the boatswain's a good seaman but in the circumstances I can't leave him to it. I'm sending an executive officer with the doctor. You.'

'Me, sir?'

'You're the most experienced, Cameron. You can take a party with you, say a leading hand and three to replace crew casualties. Volunteers to be called for in the first place. The tanker will need a full muster of seaman to handle the tow if anything goes wrong.'

'I'll see to it,' Cameron said. He turned away and left the bridge. On the iron deck he got hold of the buffer and had the word passed for volunteers. There were quite a few; most surprising of all was Leading Seaman Dewhurst. That caused a dilemma in Cameron's mind. He understood: Dewhurst wanted to get away from the ship, from his messmates, at any cost. Possibly he also saw a chance of his proving himself. But there was going to be no room for passengers or leading rates who made a hash of things. Brutally, Cameron said as much.

'I'll be all right, sir,' Dewhurst said.

Cameron studied his face closely. To turn him down might finish him off altogether. On a level of humanity he had to be given a chance; and Cameron made up his mind knowing well enough that he might be making a big mistake. On the other hand the tanker's boatswain would have all the knowledge and authority that was necessary. 'All right, Dewhurst, I'll take you,' Cameron said. He caught the eye of Leading Seaman York, who had also volunteered. York was looking sardonic: his expression said clearly, that's gone and torn it, now we've all had it.

The seaboat was called away and the boarding party with the Surgeon Lieutenant embarked at the falls. The boat was slipped from the disengaging gear and pulled across towards the jumping ladder rigged aft on the tanker's port side. Cameron went up first, to be taken and assisted over the bulwarks by the boatswain himself. Then the doctor, followed by Dewhurst and three able seamen, one of them carrying a rolled-up Neil Robinson stretcher. They all went to the bridge. Captain Harcourt had not been moved pending the arrival of the doctor: Gutteridge had been responsible for that.

He said, 'Rudimentary first aid, Doctor. Don't move an injured man. Did I do right?'

'Absolutely right,' Fleming said. He squatted on the bridge deck alongside Harcourt, who was unconscious. There was a gash along the left side of his head and there was a stomach wound as well, a nasty one. Something had gone right through to the spine. Fleming's examination didn't take long. Getting to his feet he said, 'We'll get him in the stretcher— very, very carefully. Take him to his cabin.' His face was serious.

Cameron asked, 'What's the extent of the wounds?'

'I don't know the full story of that yet.'

'Bad?'

Fleming nodded. 'All I can say is, where there's life there's hope.' He didn't, in fact, sound at all hopeful. Cameron thought about the son. Just before he'd left the destroyer Midshipman Harcourt had approached him and asked if he could board the tanker as well. Cameron had referred the request to the Captain, who had sent for Harcourt to come to the bridge.

Fanshawe had said, 'I'm sorry, Mid. Very sorry. But you know as well as I do that in the service close relatives—two brothers say—are not normally drafted to the same ship. The reason's obvious. You have a mother, haven't you?'

160

'Yes, sir.'

'Then I must think of her. So must you.'

That was all; there had been no need to stress what might happen. Fanshawe had no doubt been right; at any rate, so it had seemed at the time. Now, Cameron felt that a change of mind wouldn't be a bad thing. He believed Fleming didn't think Captain Harcourt was going to last. But he was also convinced that Fanshawe wouldn't change his mind. There was not time now for any more to-ing and fro-ing by boat between the two ships. As the Captain was taken below in the Neil Robinson stretcher carried by four men of his own crew, Cameron looked round the bridge. All was shipshape: the dead had been removed and the deck washed down already. He got the story from Gutteridge, a man of a little over forty by the look of him, a square, no-nonsense seaman with a direct manner and a formidable jaw. They had all been on the bridge, he said, out on the wings or in the wheelhouse with the quartermaster. The Italian aircraft had zoomed straight for them, raking the bridge with its cannon. Chief Officer, Second and Third Officers, they'd died instantly. The Fourth Officer had been caught on the ladder, taken in the back, and died in writhing agony a couple of minutes later. The quartermaster had got away with it, but not so the four deckhands trained as merchant gunners who had been manning the machine-guns in the

161

bridge wings and on monkey's-island on top of the wheelhouse. It had been a clean sweep of almost everyone who had been on deck, and it had left a problem behind it: the disposal of the bodies. There was canvas aboard and Gutteridge knew how to use a sailmaker's palm and needle, but Cameron was reluctant to put the dead over the side in the confused sea that might lift them and swill them aft to impact against the torpedo and shift it. For now they would have to go in the tanker's cold store for eventual committal to the deep or a shore burial in Malta.

In the wheelhouse the voice-pipe from the Master's sleeping cabin whistled. Gutteridge answered it, nodded, closed the cover and looked at Cameron.

'From the doctor,' he said briefly. 'Not much he can do except dope him down.'

'I'm sorry.'

'Yes. So am I. He's been a good skipper to sail under. Son's in your ship, I believe.'

'That's right.'

'Ought to have been sent over.'

Cameron tried to explain; the boatswain brushed the explanations aside. 'Navy's too hidebound. Too much bull. Now I suppose the Wavy Navy's in charge aboard here.' He looked at Cameron's RNVR stripes.

'I hope you don't resent it,' Cameron said.

Gutteridge laughed. 'No. Not all that much. Just so long as you don't do anything that

162

doesn't suit a merchant ship. Remember things are different.'

'Different but the same.'

Gutteridge narrowed his eyes. 'How's that?'

'We're all on the same sea. A ship's a ship. I'm here to help out, that's all.'

'More than that, Mister, while the Captain's sick. You're in command. I've sailed in convoy before. We're a naval responsibility. If you show me you know your job, I'll go along with you.'

Cameron smiled and held out his hand. 'You can't say fairer than that,' he said. Gutteridge took the hand and smiled back, then went down the starboard ladder. Cameron looked across at Dewhurst, who had accompanied him to the bridge. He said, 'Go down with the boatswain, Dewhurst. Report to him for orders. Anything he wants done, I'll expect you to see to it.'

*   *   *

Gutteridge summed up Dewhurst fairly quickly: bloody useless. Lah-de-dah voice with nothing much to back it. You didn't hear that sort of voice much aboard the merchant ships that had been Gutteridge's life from the age of fourteen. He'd started off in tramp ships— Smith's of Cardiff. From there he'd gone into the Port Line. By the time he was twenty there wasn't a lot of the world he hadn't seen, not

163

many fights he hadn't won. Life was hard, very hard, in the fo'c'sle of a merchant ship. Rated AB, with a lifeboatsman's certificate to give him an edge over the others, Gutteridge had got on. At twenty-four he'd been boatswain of a cargo-liner; he'd tinkered for a while with the notion that he might sit for a second mate's certificate of competency, but he'd given up that idea. He couldn't cope with the bookwork. An excellent practical seaman who knew his own worth, he had no ability to answer written examination questions nor to cope with *vivas* where some crusted Board of Trade examiner posed theoretical situations such as what did you do when the bottom of your ship dropped out. And navigation was a closed book to him: that took learning.

Moving with Leading Seaman Dewhurst along the flying bridge, the narrow walkway that ran the length of the ship above the tank deck, Gutteridge closed one nostril with a big thumb and blew to leeward through the other. He wondered what the BOT examiners would say if you asked *them* the question: what do you do if you've got a torpedo wedged up your arse? Thinking of this, he gave a sudden laugh.

Dewhurst said, 'I beg your pardon?'

'Granted.'

Dewhurst looked baffled. He thought there must have been something funny somewhere, but he couldn't see it. To cover his embarrassment he asked, 'How secure are the tank tops?'

'How secure? Very secure. Doesn't mean you can muck about with 'em.'

'What if there was fire on deck?'

Gutteridge grinned and said, 'Bang. There could be vapour around. Funny things, tanks. Full or empty—till they've been washed and the vapour got rid of.'

Dewhurst nodded and without thinking fished in the pocket of his white shorts and brought out a packet of Players, followed by a box of matches. 'Smoke?' he asked politely.

'Not here. Nor do you.' Gutteridge reached out and took hold of the cigarettes and matches. His voice was harsh, the boatswain's authority coming through. 'I just said, there could be vapour around. Didn't you hear me?'

'Yes—'

'Know something?'

'What?'

'You want to acquire some common sense. Smoke anywhere aboard here except in the crew's smoking room and I'll kick you in the balls, so help me. You'd better tell your mates that too.'

Dewhurst flushed. 'I'm awfully sorry, Mr Gutteridge.'

'Don't call me Mister. I'm not an officer. Just call me boatswain.'

Dewhurst nodded. Gutteridge went on with his explanatory tour of the ship, explained the working of the windlass that, situated abaft the break of the fo'c'sle, took the place in merchant ships of the centre-line capstan and cable-holders used aboard warships for working the cable. Gutteridge outlined the system of tanks: *British Racer* stowed her six-million gallon cargo in nine sets of tanks, all except one being composed of a main centre tank carrying 391,500 gallons of high octane aviation spirit with another 165,000 gallons in each of two side tanks to port and starboard; the remaining set consisted of just side tanks. All these were separated longitudinally by strong bulkheads, and there were pump rooms situated fore and aft.

'As you can see,' Gutteridge said, 'we're big. Five hundred and twenty-three feet overall length, sixty-eight in the beam, thirty foot loaded draught. Doesn't make for easy handling.'

From the fo'c'sle-head Dewhurst looked aft towards the bridge superstructure containing the deck officers' accommodation. It was a long vista of steel deck interspersed with the tank tops. Abaft the midship island there was the same again, till you met the poop. The *British Racer* was immense compared with the *Burnside*. So far as the RN was concerned only the battleships, battle-cruisers and aircraft carriers were bigger. But the tanker, deeply loaded, stood low in the water; very little freeboard. As the wind increased and brought the sea up, waves began to come inboard and

166

wash across the deck, breaking against the tank tops and sending up spray. The walk aft was a wet one. Dewhurst was visualizing two things during that walk: the thousands of tons of aviation spirit beneath him, moving sluggishly in the full tanks—and the possible movement of that torpedo against the ship's side as the now turbulent sea surged around it.

Suddenly, he felt overwhelming fear. He wondered why he had volunteered. But it was too late now.

*   *   *

A watch was being maintained on the tanker's fo'c'sle-head, a watch on the tow. At any moment it might be necessary to pay out cable to ease undue strain. Dewhurst and the three able seamen from the *Burnside* shared the watch with the tanker's crew. Gutteridge had put Dewhurst on early, so that he could gain some sort of experience of judging the strain while the ship was moving through peaceful water and in daylight. Cameron looked down from the bridge, saw Dewhurst standing a prudent distance away from the links of the cable. If the cable parted the chances were it would fall slack; it wasn't like a steel-wire hawser, it hadn't the spring. But if it was not eased in time and the pull tore out one of the slips, then anyone close by stood a fair chance of being killed or at least seriously injured.

167

Dewhurst seemed to have enough seamanship, at any rate in a self-preservative sense, to know all that.

From *Burnside*'s quarterdeck Leading Seaman York also saw Dewhurst up there in the tanker's bows. 'Stone the crows,' he said in mock amazement to the buffer. 'Mr Cameron must be off his bleedin' rocker.'

'Why?'

York pointed. 'Look, Buff.'

PO Burnett looked. 'Oh, yes,' he said, wiping the back of a hand across his nose. 'One thing, he's far enough off that tin fish, not that it'll do him any good.'

'Ah,' York said sagely, 'but at least 'e can't do *it* no bloody 'arm.' He paused. 'What's going to 'appen about 'is 'ook, do you know, Buff? That charge.'

'I don't know a thing,' Burnett said. 'Not up to me.'

York sniffed and thumped a fist on the barrel of his gun. Bloody Dewhurst. His mind shifted to more practical matters: there had been no time since leaving Scapa to get any dhobying done and he felt not far off being lousy. He'd worn his socks and under-pants for almost a fortnight, night and day. They almost stood up on their own. Then there was Beano and what was left of the litter. Took time, looking after the cat. It was all go. Bugger the war. Suddenly York felt a shiver run along his spine for no reason at all. A moment later he assumed he must have had a premonition; the tannoy came on and Fanshawe's voice said, without any stress of emotion or anything else to show he was human, 'The ship is about to enter the channel through the deep minefield.'

That was all; the tannoy clicked off. York thought, why can't the silly bugger call it the Gap like anyone else? He gave a hitch to his trousers; they always felt as if they were about to slip and never mind that he wore braces as well as his seaman's money-belt. Must be something to do with his gut.

*   *   *

By now, as the three ships moved slowly into the narrows, the *British Racer* was yawing about badly, putting a strain on the tow. The wind was up to around Force 7 or 8 on the Beaufort Scale and more water was surging across the tanks. If it got much worse they would be main deck awash, with only the fo'c'sle and the bridge superstructure and the poop standing clear. Cameron reckoned they could do with two ships on the tow again, but it was too late for that now. The Gap was no place for that sort of manoeuvre and no doubt Fanshawe still wanted to feel free vis-à-vis enemy attack.

Gutteridge joined Cameron on the bridge. He said, 'News isn't good about the Captain. I just spoke to his steward. He's only just about

169

hanging on.'

'We're not all that far off Malta. They'll have him into Bighi as soon as we enter.'

'Be too late, I reckon, Mister.'

'Let's hope not. How's the cable?'

'Not too happy. Surging about when she yaws. But it's been well maintained, no weak spots. Don't know about yours.'

Cameron said, 'We ranged cable in the Clyde not long ago. In the Admiralty floating dock. It should be all right.'

They watched out together. There was little for anyone to do other than watch—and be ready to act on the instant. The ship, with the Not Under Control balls hoisted, round, black and somehow sinister, from the starboard fore upper yard, was inert and helpless without her engines, without her own steering. It was a frustrating command to have thrust upon him, Cameron felt. He didn't relish the feeling of the mines, so close, comparatively, on either hand. Mines could break loose, especially in bad weather, be a floating menace. Fanshawe had thought of that; Dewhurst and the two able seamen had rifles with them, and Cameron was equipped with a revolver. Another revolver had been brought from the Master's safe. On the bridge and fo'c'sle there was a mine watch. If a mine was sighted, they would aim for one of its horns and blow it up—always assuming it hadn't come too close before it was seen.

170

A few minutes later the tanker's radio officer came with a weather report: there was a force 9 gale ahead. The report was a little superfluous. The wind was getting heavier by the minute already. Spindrift was blowing back from the bows, flinging over the bridge, covering the tank deck with mist. There was a hollow booming from aft as heavier waves crashed into the hull. Cameron glanced at the boatswain.

'Engine spaces,' Gutteridge said briefly. 'Full tanks don't make that racket.'

'I hope that torpedo isn't reacting.'

'I'm doing my best not to think about it,' Gutteridge said. He took up a pair of binoculars; he was using Captain Harcourt's. He had stiffened and was about to utter when a shout came back along the wind from Dewhurst in the bows.

'*Aircraft bearing red nine-oh, sir!*'

Cameron picked up the bearing quickly. Stukas, and plenty of them. Now the crunch was coming. Gutteridge ran out of the wheelhouse and Cameron heard him climbing the ladder to monkey's-island and the machine-guns. Two of the tanker's crew came up the ladder from the Master's deck and ran to the machine-guns in the bridge wings. Cameron remained with the quartermaster, still on the wheel for form's sake, the wheel that stood lashed to prevent any movement of the telemotor gear that might turn the rudder, however slightly, against the trapped torpedo. For the first time Cameron noticed the tattoos on the man's forearms: one said *I love Carmen*, with, across it, another tattoo reading *cancelled*. An obvious indiscretion in South America.

The Stukas roared in. As two of them peeled off into a dive, the machine-guns stuttered out and spent cartridge cases rattled on the bridge deck.

*   *   *

Burnside and *Brahmin* were sending up the by now customary barrage. The guns' crews were practised at it by this time and reacted automatically. Two of the Stukas were hit early on, one of them by a sheer fluke while it was still high, before it had gone into its screaming death-dive. It twisted, and a wing fluttered down. Then it went into a sickening spiral and crashed into the sea, well off to starboard. There was a monumental explosion. On *Burnside*'s bridge Fanshawe said, 'They've set off a mine. More than one, perhaps.'

He watched as the disturbed water, heaved up like the dome of St Paul's, fell back again. All around the ships more upheavals were taking place as the bombs fell; the hulls rang like bells. This time it seemed as though the Stukas meant to make a job of it. Doggedly the tow went on, moving slowly between the

172

bombs. The first casualties came from the Stukas' machine-guns: *Brahmin*'s upper deck was raked and the radar aerials were shattered into useless metal cats'cradles. Next was a near miss, a bomb that exploded on impact with the sea close to the *Burnside* and sent her lurching sideways. The force of so close an explosion blew the gunner's mate over the side. He was uninjured but dazed; when he came through the shock he saw the ships moving away from him. He waved an arm and shouted hoarsely, but the ships moved on. The arm still waved, the hand now forming a fist.

'Bastards!' PO Garter screamed. 'Dirty bastards!' He could have been yelling at the Stukas; he could have been yelling at those who were leaving him behind. There was a sob in his throat but gunnery discipline, gunnery toughness, was still in charge. He swam. The ships were making only around four knots, he believed. In point of fact Fanshawe had increased the speed of the tow, taking a chance on straining it. Even another couple of knots could help. The gunner's mate couldn't make it; instead, he dropped back towards the tanker coming on astern of *Brahmin*.

Leading Seaman Dewhurst spotted him and called the bridge. Cameron, notionally in command but in fact a spare hand, raced down the ladders to the tank deck and freed the rolled-up jumping ladder, sent it cascading down to the waterline, together with a

173

lifebuoy. Gasping, the gunner's mate got an arm through the lifebuoy and struck out for the foot of the jumping ladder. He heaved himself up, hung for a long moment getting his breath and strength back, then climbed to the deck.

Cameron helped him over. PO Garter shook water from his white uniform like a dog. He was white-faced and shivery but he was still a gunner's mate. Capless, he saluted. 'Thank you, sir. Come aboard to join, sir—in a manner of speaking, that is.' As fast as possible Cameron helped him along the deck and up the ladders to the officers' accommodation. He took him to the first cabin he came across, which was that of the late Second Officer. In it he found a bottle of whisky. He said, 'Help yourself.'

'Thank you, sir. I will. Then I'm taking charge of the guns. If you can call them that. Machine-guns against soddin' Stukas, it's crazy.' Suddenly he gave a wince, and staggered, then sat down sharply. He said, 'It's me back, sir. Nothing to worry about. Touch of lumbago, I reckon.'

Back on the bridge, Cameron felt his nails digging into his palms. *Burnside*'s upper deck was a shambles of twisted metal, and fire had broken out amidships. Men were running everywhere, a kind of controlled bedlam. As Cameron watched, a stick of bombs took the *Brahmin*, straight as a die along her upper

174

deck from for'ard to aft. There was an almighty explosion—a series of explosions. As the depth charges went up there was a sheet of flame and a pall of smoke. When the smoke cleared, there was little left except fire and debris. The upper deck was flat, all the superstructure gone. It was almost impossible to say where the bridge had been. From the tanker's bows the tow had fallen slack, straight up-and-down from the fairleads: it had been blown off at the other end, freed by the bombs from the destroyer's quarterdeck. Dewhurst and one of the merchant seamen were getting the windlass in motion, attempting to heave in the cable. *Burnside* was standing off to starboard, still putting up a barrage. So far the *British Racer* was unharmed; the Stukas had evidently decided to concentrate on the warships and put all their guns out of action before blowing up the tanker.

Garter climbed the ladders from the cabin flat, stiffly, in agony now from his spine. But determined to fight back ... reaching the bridge, he went on up to monkey's-island. When he reached the high platform something seemed to give, to snap. A tendon or something, or a back muscle, he wouldn't know. What he did know was that he couldn't stand upright and the bloke on one of the machine-guns hadn't much of an idea how best to use it.

Garter moved across the deck, bent almost

175

double, an old age pensioner long before his time. Reaching the gun he said harshly, 'Leave it.'

Gutteridge turned to look. 'Who the hell might you be?'

'Name of Garter. Gunner's mate aboard the *Burnside*. Give the gun to me, all right?'

'Bugger off,' Gutteridge said, and turned back to squeeze the trigger again.

'For Christ's sake! You're wasting ammo, mate. Best hold your fire till it can do some bloody good. Gunnery's my job, see? I don't know who you are, but you're no bloody gunner, that's for sure.'

Gutteridge said, 'Bollocks.' A Stuka was coming in, a screaming dive towards the *Burnside*. Garter moved as fast as he could for the second gun. Gutteridge aimed, squeezed, and was dead lucky. The Stuka went into a spin. There was no doubt that it had been Gutteridge who had got the target; the tracer had been seen, going slap into the cockpit and the pilot. Gutteridge looked round, grinning and streaming sweat despite the chill that was now in the air. 'See that, did you?'

'Fuck a duck,' Garter said. His back was giving him hell now. He couldn't help it: he dropped to the deck. He would need to be winched down, the ladder was out. From his recumbent position he saw the next Stuka coming in viciously. It looked as if it was the *British Racer*'s turn at last. The Stuka's dive flattened and the bombs came down. They all proved near misses, except one. There was an explosion aft and fire broke out in the tanker's stern. The bomb had gone slap into the engineers' and deckhands' accommodation in the poop.

CHAPTER TWELVE

Gutteridge shook a fist in the air, yelling defiance and hate. The attack was breaking off; a case either of all bombs gone or enough damage done. The tanker couldn't last now—that would be the thought in the squadron commander's mind. The boatswain turned for the ladder, saw Garter lying in a heap. 'You hit?' he asked.

'No. Me bloody back, that's all—'

Gutteridge bent. 'I'll get you below.'

Garter said, 'Don't worry about me, worry about the fire.' Gutteridge took no notice. He lifted the gunner's mate easily, slung him across his shoulder and went down the vertical ladder with him. On the bridge, he laid him gently on the coconut matting in the wheelhouse. There was no one else there; in a powerless ship the bridge was of less importance than the fire, and Cameron had already gone aft.

Gutteridge went aft as well. The hoses were

out and the hands were playing them on the flames, on the red-hot metal of the deckhouse; along the tank tops the sea was still washing over and that could be their salvation.

Cameron remarked on this as the boatswain joined him from the flying bridge. Gutteridge said, 'Maybe, yes. Maybe, no. If the fire has gone deep the heat could reach the tanks through the coffer-dam and after pump-room. Know about the flash point, do you?'

Cameron nodded; the flash point was the temperature to which an oil cargo had to be heated so as to give off vapour in enough quantity to be ignited by a flame when mixed with air. Gutteridge went on, 'With spirit, the flash point's below 75 degrees Fahrenheit. There's also the ignition point. That's when the surface layers go on fire. It's tricky.' He wiped sweat from his eyes. The air was like a furnace. 'Know what the casualties are in that lot, do you?'

'Not yet. But I doubt if anyone had much chance.'

'Likely not. I'm going to take a look at the pump-room.' Gutteridge turned away. Removing his shirt he balled it up, wetted it with sea-water, and held it over his nose and mouth. Then he went in through the entry to the after superstructure, vanishing from sight. Above him the shattered metal glowed red. The water from the hoses was turned to steam in the instant it hit the superstructure.

Unshackled now from the tow, the *British Racer* drifted.

*   *   *

Fanshawe's face was grey. The wind, blowing strongly, had backed a little and was coming from the north-east. Fanshawe said with a note of desperation, 'She'll be blown into the minefield if it goes on this way.' There were just three things he could do: one, he could back up to the tanker's bows and grapple her cable, shackle on a wire hawser and take up the tow in place of the sunken *Brahmin*. Two, he could place his ship where it could nudge the *British Racer* away from the minefield, like a berthing tug in Portsmouth harbour nudging a battleship into the South Railway jetty. It would be a tricky job in the weather they were getting. Three, he could order Cameron to abandon, pick up the Naval party and the ship's crew, and make all speed possible into Malta. It was a captain's duty to make the decision and make it fast. Fanshawe was inclined towards the third choice. The first alternative would take too long, and his ship's company was fully occupied in fighting the fire amidships. That bomb had done plenty of damage; one of the casualties had been his cable, ranged along the deck ready for the precise purpose of taking up the tow if *Brahmin* should be put out of action or if the

179

tow needed double-banking. He could bring out the other cable but that would take even more time and manpower.

He glanced at Harcourt. The midshipman, Officer of the Watch in place of the RNVR sub-lieutenant who had been killed in the recent attack, was in a state of nervous tension and no wonder. A badly wounded father in a ship that couldn't last long was no one's idea of joy. And Fanshawe, whatever his duty might dictate, found he had no stomach for an order to abandon a man who, by the sound of the doctor's signalled report earlier, would be highly unlikely to survive the ordeal of a transfer at sea in the prevailing conditions.

But could that man's life be reasonably set against so many others? That one life, plus the vital necessity of getting the tanker's cargo into Malta if at all possible?

It could not.

In a controlled voice Fanshawe passed his decision to the leading signalman. 'Make to *British Racer: You are to abandon ship. I will stand by to take all hands from the water.*'

He avoided the midshipman's eye. The leading signalman began clacking out the message on a battery-fed Aldis lamp. Fanshawe turned his attention aft, where the fire parties seemed to be having some success. He saw Bartram supervising the dousing of the depth charges in the racks and throwers. Amidships the torpedo-tubes on both sides were a mangled mess; by some miracle, some kindliness on the part of unpredictable explosive, the fish hadn't gone up when the bomb had struck, but now they too were being doused with the cooling hoses as a precaution. Bartram was everywhere at once, regretting the absence of his gunner's mate but grateful enough for the TGM's assistance. Petty Officer Trent had been wounded, a splinter in his ribs, but it wasn't much and he was carrying on. Bartram hoped the doctor would soon be brought back aboard to see to the casualties, but no doubt he was needed aboard the tanker. Bartram leaned back for a moment against the after screen, feeling his age and still very sore on his backside, thanks to bloody Musso. He was sweating like a pig and breathing like a God knew what, grampus. He felt very far from well all of a sudden.

It was Leading Seaman York who saw the gunner slide down the bulkhead and crumple in a heap on the deck. He ran for him, saw the staring eyes, felt for the heart. No beats so far as he could tell. He sent an OD down to the medical dressing station with an urgent message to the LSBA. Trott came up as soon as he could make it. He bent and examined the gunner, then looked up. 'Dead,' he said.

York asked blankly, 'What of? No bloody wounds.'

The LSBA shrugged. 'Could be a heart attack.' York shook his head sadly. Poor old

181

bugger, notwithstanding that he'd once been a gunner's mate, he'd been a decent sort.

On the bridge Fanshawe was growing impatient. He rounded on the leading signalman. 'Haven't you got that signal through yet?'

'Not answering, sir. There's no one on the bridge, I reckon, sir. All aft.' Then the leading signalman's tone changed. 'They're making to us, sir. Someone there after all.' There was a pause, then he said, *'From British Racer, Lieutenant Cameron, fire coming under control, sir.'*

'I see. In—'

'More coming through, sir. *Request tow be taken up*, sir.'

Fanshawe nodded. He could scarcely pass the order to abandon now. He said, 'Make to Lieutenant Cameron: *I shall pass a tow as soon as possible. Meanwhile I propose to push you clear of the minefield.'*

'Aye, aye, sir.'

'Harcourt, take the ship to the tanker's starboard side. Engines half ahead.'

The midshipman acknowledged the order and bent to the voice-pipe. *Burnside* swung as the coxswain put the helm over. Below in the engine-room Mr Canton watched the seepage of water—it was more than a seepage now—and clicked his tongue in concern. They were being hard put to it now to keep the water-level down, as he had already reported to the skipper. That last attack hadn't done the sprung plates any good at all. There was water elsewhere too and the ship was starting to feel sluggish and inert. And it was still a long way to Malta. When the word came down from the bridge informing the engine-room of what Fanshawe proposed to do, Mr Canton gave a grimace. You had to do everything you could, of course; but from now on they were going to be slap alongside that torpedo's potential.

* * *

The Chief Engineer was alive, plus just one junior engineer and a greaser. The apparent miracle was due to the fact that they had all been down in the for'ard pump-room when the bomb had hit; and they joined Cameron from for'ard just after Gutteridge had plunged suicidally into the after superstructure. Later, once the fire was out and the metal cooling to the liberal supply of water from the hoses, it had become possible to look, however hopelessly, for survivors.

There had been none. The smell had been terrible; the whole after superstructure was a crematorium. But there was one bright spot for what it might be worth: the bomb—it couldn't have been one of the really big ones— hadn't penetrated to the engine-room, or anyway the Chief Engineer was reasonably satisfied that it hadn't. The decking above the engine spaces was, he believed, intact; the explosive force had been soaked up by the accommodation. Badly shaken, Cameron went back to the bridge, looked down at the destroyer now pushing against the side plating below the midship superstructure, surging dangerously up and down, her bullring already bent out of shape and the tanker's side dented. It was murder on paintwork but this was no time to think about the niceties of tiddley ships. If the weather worsened the nudging attempt must be doomed to failure. Cameron thought about Gutteridge, who had not reappeared. It was impossible to say whether or not the boatswain had ever reached the pump-room; there was no possibility of reaching it to take a look. While the fire had been at its height the after superstructure had collapsed inwards and the inspection after the metal had cooled had shown that the hatch to the after pump-room lay beneath a mass of tangled metal.

Close alongside now, Fanshawe used his loud hailer to call up. 'By my reckoning we're very close to the minefield and it's touch and go.' He managed a bleak smile. 'Literally! How's that torpedo?'

'Still there, sir, so far as I know. How about reconnecting the tow?'

Fanshawe gave a shrug. 'We're going to need room between you and the minefield on both sides—it's going to take time to pass the tow and once I come away from your side you'll drift. I suggest you send a man down to look at your torpedo.'

'Aye, aye, sir.' Cameron hesitated. 'May *I* make a suggestion, sir?'

'Go ahead.'

'Why not break wireless silence, sir? Hasten the rescue tug ... if Rear-Admiral(D) hasn't reached Malta yet, they won't know—'

'Yes, yes. I've considered that. I don't like it. The enemy may be thinking they've sunk us and if so I don't want to disillusion them by transmitting. In any case I have to assume they can crack our cypher, in which case any such signal would be likely to ensure that a tug would never reach us.' Fanshawe paused. 'Now, that torpedo.'

He switched off. Cameron turned away. On the deck of the wheelhouse the gunner's mate seemed more or less comfortable but was feeling the indignity of being a literal layabout. Gunner's mates never draped themselves on the deck. As Leading Seaman Dewhurst came along the flying bridge from aft, Cameron called to him. He and two of the able seamen were to tend a line while he, Cameron, went over the side to take a look at the torpedo. Dewhurst had just gone aft again on his errand when the Surgeon Lieutenant came up from the Master's deck.

He said, 'He hasn't long to go. I think you'd better tell Fanshawe.'

185

'You're thinking of the mid?'

Fleming nodded. 'Yes. Harcourt's well doped down and probably won't recognize him. But all the same . . .'

'I take your point,' Cameron said. He walked into the wing and looked down again at *Burnside*'s bridge. The mid was there with the Captain: an awkward message had to be passed. Cameron called down, 'Captain, sir.'

'Yes?'

'Could you spare the midshipman, sir?'

'What?'

'Just for a while, sir.'

Fanshawe opened his mouth then seemed to understand. He said, 'Very well, Cameron. Send a jumping ladder down to my fo'c'sle.'

'Aye, aye, sir.' There were no hands available; Cameron went down himself to the after tank deck and unsecured the jumping ladder, dragging the heavy weight a little way for'ard until it was over the destroyer's bows. Making the inboard end fast, he dropped the ladder down to the fo'c'sle, where Harcourt was waiting. The midshipman scrambled aboard and saluted.

'You wanted me, sir?'

'Your father, Mid.'

Harcourt paled. 'Has he . . . died?'

'No. The doc's doing his best. He just thought your father might want to see you.'

'Yes, I see. What you mean is, he's not going to live.'

186

Cameron said, 'I'm bloody sorry, Mid. No one can say he's not going to live, though. He's in his cabin,' he added. 'Better get along there.'

The midshipman turned away and went fast up the ladder to the midships superstructure. Cameron went aft to where Dewhurst was waiting with the line. The sea was slapping against the plates; he doubted if the disturbed water would allow him to see much if anything, but Fanshawe had given the order and the attempt had to be made. With the line secured beneath his arm-pits he climbed the bulwarks and was lowered to the waterline. Aboard the destroyer, not far for'ard of where Cameron was being lowered, Leading Seaman York watched Dewhurst at work on the lifeline and gave a guffaw. Mr Cameron, he *must* be off his nut. Just fancy trusting one's life to bloody Dewhurst! As good as suicide, that was. Dewhurst couldn't even look after a ship's cat properly, daft clot.

Cameron had been right: he could see nothing from the surface. Like Captain Harcourt earlier, he called up to be lowered further and he went under, right down deep, feeling the pressure. Just below him he saw the torpedo. It wasn't stationary now, it was swaying with the movement of the water, slowly, ponderously, its lethal nose no longer visible. Cameron probed with his foot, taking a risk. He made contact, and pushed. It was very

187

solid despite the sway; it was still trapped somewhere farther down, out of sight. Cameron tugged on the rope and was pulled as far as the surface. He took several gasps of air, then went down again, deeper. This time he saw the small propellers that gave the torpedo its motion. *Tail end in view* . . .

Somehow or other the thing had managed to reverse itself while still held fast. The nose must be pointing down towards the foot of the rudder-post. There had never been any hope that the firing-pin could be removed in the time a man could hold his breath and do a delicate job, and if there had been it had gone now. If the fish blew, it wouldn't just blow through the ship's side. It would blow along the bottom plating directly below the tanks. The double-bottoms would be no more protection than cardboard.

Back on deck, Cameron climbed to the bridge where he had a word with Garter. Fleming was there with him; the gunner's mate was in obvious pain but doing his best to make light of what he thought of as a daft injury, one not attributable to action except indirectly. He had refused to go below: felt safer up top, he said. He listened to what Cameron had to say, then gave his opinion. 'I don't reckon it makes much difference, sir. If that fish hits any part of the ship, we're all goners. You say it's still wedged fast, sir?'

'Yes. So far as I could see, it's sort of nipped

by its propellers.'

'What by, sir? I mean what's nipping the props?'

'The rudder, I think.'

'That's odd.' Garter rasped at his cheeks, frowning. 'I suppose the rudder could have moved a bit, in spite of the lashed wheel. In any case, sir, there's sod all we can do about it.'

Cameron nodded. There were other things he should be thinking about. PO Garter for one: he was no use aboard the tanker and should be lifted back to the *Burnside* in a Neil Robinson stretcher. On the other hand the dangers, with *Burnside* nudging close to the tanks, would be little different if the worst happened. There was another thing: what were any of them doing aboard the *British Racer* now? She was out of all control and they might just as well abandon, and try to save the tanker and its cargo by remote control as it were—by shifting aboard the destroyer and keeping the big ship out in the deep channel.

But that was up to Fanshawe.

On his bridge, Fanshawe's thoughts were running along similar lines. For the second time he was about to order the men off the tanker when the starboard lookout reported aircraft coming in from the east. Cursing the fact that his radar had gone in the earlier attack, Fanshawe swung his bonoculars onto the bearing.

Six aircraft . . . no, seven.

Fanshawe stiffened, staring in disbelief. Incredulously he said, his voice high, 'They're ours! God Almighty! Six Seafires and a Beaufighter ...' A cheer went up along the bedraggled decks as the familiar British silhouettes were recognized, and steel helmets were waved. The Seafires flew low over the two ships, the pilots waving back. The Beaufighter passed more distantly along the port side, making a signal by lamp, difficult enough to read from a fast aircraft.

Fanshawe's signalman reported, 'Rescue tug on its way with divers, sir.'

Fanshawe took off his tin hat and waved it above his head in acknowledgement and heartfelt thanks. He read into the message that the Malta detachment of the convoy had arrived somewhat ahead of its ETA with the Admiral's request for a tug, and that one of the carriers had flown off the aircraft outside the Grand Harbour. Fanshawe passed the word down and it spread fast throughout the ship and there was more cheering. Spirits shot high now; they had all known that the tug would eventually be sent, but it was immensely heartening to have the confirmation, to know that it was really on its way. The aircraft flew away again, back towards Malta. The fact they'd been in contact was enough for Fanshawe. His position would be known now. Seafires couldn't remain in the air for long, but as from now the fleet would be ready to give cover and when another attack came in Fanshawe wouldn't hesitate to break wireless silence. In the meantime he would not leave the *British Racer* without a crew. There must be men aboard to take the tow from the rescue tug and the two ships could become separated by the weather before the tug's arrival. Already the nudging business was a hazard and *Burnside*'s bow was crumpled from the constant impacting against the tanker's side as she laboured to the sea.

Fanshawe, using his loud hailer, called across to Cameron, passing the report of the rescue tug. He asked, 'Have you enough hands to take the tow?'

'Probably not,' Cameron answered. Almost all the tanker's own crew had died in the explosion of the bomb aft—all except those manning the machine-guns. 'I could do with six more seamen, sir. In the circumstances.'

Fanshawe nodded: he knew what Cameron meant. If it hadn't been for the promise of the rescue tug he wouldn't have wanted to put more men at risk. Switching off the loud hailer, Fanshawe passed the word for more volunteers. Leading Seaman York was one. Petty Officer Trent was another; his torpedo-tubes now gone, Fanshawe felt able to spare him. With four able seamen and ordinary seamen they were put aboard the tanker. Fanshawe watched them go; he was filled with misgivings. Surely, before long, the sea's

191

movement was going to drive that torpedo's nose into something solid. The fact that it had been swaying about gave no one any cause for complacency.

*   *   *

The weather worsened; there came a moment when Fanshawe knew that he couldn't hope to hold the tanker with his nudging bows and that the time had come to make an attempt to pass another tow. It would be difficult and it would have to be done fast. With the thrust of the destroyer withdrawn, the *British Racer* could do nothing but move with the wind towards the fringe of the minefield. Fanshawe made the decision not to range another cable along his decks; simply, it would take far too long. A plain towing pendant of steel wire with a rope spring would have to be used; and they would have to hope and pray that it would hold until the rescue tug arrived.

He passed his intentions to Cameron. While preparations were made aboard the tanker and his own ship, Fanshawe kept his ship in position, trying to hold his bows hard against the plates while his bow scraped up and down to the lift and scend of the seas. He watched Trent and York making their way for'ard along the flying bridge with the hands. The tanker's carpenter, luckily one of the survivors, was at the windlass, all ready to pass the destroyer's

192

wire round the drums and heave in—always provided anyone could catch a heaving-line with this wind blowing. But York was a good man; if anyone could catch it, he would.

From the tanker's bridge, Cameron reported ready.

Fanshawe waved an arm in acknowledgement. He called up, 'I'm going astern now. I'll come round and drop down on your bows, all right?'

'Yes, sir.'

Fanshawe spoke down the voice-pipe. 'Engines half astern, wheel amidships.'

The destroyer backed away.

* * *

York said suddenly, 'We'll never make it. We'll never bloody make it, not a hope in hell.'

'Make what?' Trent asked. 'Malta?'

York jeered. 'Sure we'll never make bloody Malta! But I meant the tow. Stands to reason. It's against nature. Look at the sea.'

Trent said, 'We've *got* to make it. Skipper knows what he's doing, and young Cameron, he's all right too.' Always the optimist; but it was true enough, it was going to be shaky. It was far from towing weather, but on the other hand it had been done before now. Trent had read reports in the papers, back before the war, of ships adrift in the Atlantic gales, ships that had had a tow passed, ships that had got back into port somehow or other. Never say die, was Trent's motto and he didn't think it was a bad one. He'd been in some tricky spots in his time: typhoons on the old China station, in a light cruiser rolling her gunwales under beneath a shrieking wind; a County class cruiser that had broached-to in the Great Australian Bight, battered by winds blowing straight up from the South Polar regions. He wasn't going to let the Med get him down. With York, he watched as the *Burnside* manoeuvred into position. York said, 'Poor old crate, eh, she's in a bleedin' awful mess. Bloody bastards! Just look at her.'

Trent did so. He and York were watching when *Burnside* hit a mine.

CHAPTER THIRTEEN

Very suddenly, Mr Canton, on the starting platform, had ceased to worry about the seepage of water through the sprung plates. There had been a tremendous roar, a tremendous concussion, and the side of the engine-room opened up like an oyster. Canton was spread like jam over the fractured steam pipes, the twisted steel ladders, the shining brass of shattered handwheels and dials and gauges. Within a matter of seconds of his death the engine-room and boiler-rooms were flooded and the ship was settling aft. Not one man got away from the engine spaces. The ship lay dead, no power left. Everywhere below decks the lights went out. In the listing wheelhouse CPO Dickens still held a useless wheel.

Fanshawe's shaken voice came down. 'Cox'n, pipe all hands on deck, stand by to abandon ship.'

'Aye, aye, sir.' Dickens found that there wasn't even power on the tannoy, so he despatched a boatswain's mate and stood by for more orders. Any moment another bloody mine might go up; they'd drifted farther than the skipper thought, unless this had been a mine that had become detached from its sinker in the heavy sea. Such things did happen, and what about that tanker if another one drifted smack into her?

Curtains. The skipper's voice came down again, sounding defeated. 'All right, Cox'n. Leave the wheelhouse, get on deck.'

'Aye, aye, sir.' Dickens passed the order to his wheelhouse staff. 'Right, outside. Looks like this is it.' He followed the seamen out into the open, having almost to climb the canted deck, and looked aft. His lips framed a whistle. She was in a bad way, was the old *Burnside*. The starboard side amidships to aft lifted and split like a sardine tin. That shocking list, and down heavily by the stern. And that dead feeling, the sickening inertness as she heaved sluggishly in the water. There was nothing the damage control parties could do now; she was beyond that. Because there had been something in the skipper's voice that seemed to say he wanted his hand held, Dickens climbed to the bridge. The skipper had been overdoing it, and was dead tired. He was probably blaming himself. Reaching Fanshawe's side, Dickens saluted.

He said, 'One of those things, sir.'

'What?' Fanshawe was staring aft as if not registering. He was alone except for the leading signalman. 'What did you say, Cox'n?'

'Nothing really, sir. Do we abandon, or what, sir?'

'I'm waiting for reports.'

'Yes, sir.' Dickens paused. 'Best not delay too long, sir.'

Fanshawe looked at him. 'You think she's going?'

'No doubt of it, sir.'

'I'm not so sure after all. I'd like to get her in, Cox'n. Get her past the breakwater. Less than a hundred miles to go now.'

'A long enough way, sir. For a sinking ship.'

'She may not be, don't you see?' Fanshawe's tone was edgy. 'She's not going any farther over. It's surprising, but she's not. You can feel that, can't you?'

Dickens pursed his lips. It was true, she wasn't. He said doubtfully, 'Watertight doors and bulkheads *could* be holding, sir. I'll nip

196

down, take a look for myself, see just what's going on.'

Fanshawe nodded without speaking. Dickens turned away and went fast down the ladder. Going aft, he met the buffer. He asked briskly, 'What's it like?'

'Not all that bad, considering, 'Swain. We have a chance. That is, unless we hit another mine.'

'You can say that again,' Dickens said, and moved on. They might, just might, be all right for a while, mines and the sea did funny things at times, but all right or not, they had no power and never would again. If the skipper had notions of any survival aboard in the long run then he was barmy. Dickens carried out as close an inspection as possible. Everything was in a bloody awful mess and he couldn't get below, but looking down through the tangle he believed thc bulkheads and watertight sections were holding—so far. God alone could say for how long, with the action of the sea pressing in through what had been the engine-room. In Dickens' view, they were best out. They could get the rafts away and paddle for the tanker and wait for the rescue tug. Some people were just obstinate; yet Dickens had to admit that they would be no better off aboard the tanker. Back on the upper deck he looked across at her; he was dead positive she was drifting closer. Minefields were no place for laden tankers. It was all up with the lot of them.

Blood drummed in Dickens' ears and he thought of home. If his missus knew the pickle he was in she would die on the spot. Going back off every leave, she'd always cried her eyes out. She always thought he was never going to come back. This time, it looked as though she'd been right.

*   *   *

From the destroyer's bridge the leading signalman was sending a message by semaphore. Slowly, Cameron read it off. *Am disabled but expect to remain afloat and do not propose to abandon.*

'For Christ's sake,' PO Trent said softly. He had come up to the bridge when all prospect of a tow had vanished. 'What *does* he expect to do, I ask you, sir!'

Cameron shrugged. There was no answer to that. There was no answer to anything in this situation; all they could do was wait. Drift, and wait, and hope for a massive stroke of luck in that they might still be alive when the rescue tug came in. All he could do was to maintain a mine watch, and that was negative enough. They couldn't do anything about it if they hit one. They could pick off floating ones by gunfire, but the hidden ones were the menace, the ones they wouldn't see until they went up in searing bloody flame ... Cameron was thinking very bleak thoughts when Leading Seaman Dewhurst came into the wheelhouse,

198

looking tense. Looking more than tense; haunted almost, and obviously screwed up to something.

He said, 'May I have a word, sir?'

'Go ahead, Dewhurst.'

'I've got a suggestion, sir.'

'All suggestions welcome!' Cameron grinned. 'Let's have it, then.'

The set look on Dewhurst's face deepened. There was real determination. He said, 'That charge, sir.'

'Charge?'

'You know, sir. What happened before Gibraltar.'

'*That* sort of charge!' Cameron blew out his breath. 'Bloody hell . . . this isn't the time to be thinking of that, Dewhurst. It's not up to me in any case, you know that—'

'Yes, sir. But it's been on my mind. I know what everyone's been saying—I've been on the sticky end of that. I don't suppose you realize what it's been like.'

Cameron said, 'I've got some idea. I was on the lower deck myself. What is it you want?'

Dewhurst moistened his lips. He was standing straight and stiff, filled with tension. He said, 'I don't know if you'll understand, sir. I was failed at *King Alfred*. If I lose my rate as leading seaman that'll be the last straw. Not so much for me. It's my father I'm thinking of . . . and what his reaction would be. He's a major-general.'

Cameron nodded. 'Yes, I know. And I understand all right, don't doubt that. Just tell me what you're asking, that's all.'

'Yes, sir.' Dewhurst paused, staring into Cameron's face. He went on, 'If we could get under way sir—'

'If's a big word, Dewhurst.'

'Yes, sir. But that's what we have to do. It's obvious. We have to take the *Burnside* in tow. If we don't . . .' He shrugged; there was no need to put it into words. 'She can't move, we *could*—if it wasn't for that torpedo.'

Cameron stared. By this time enough of the tangle of metal in the after accommodation had been cleared to allow access to the engine spaces and it had been confirmed that the engines were intact, and the Chief Engineer had reported earlier that no internal damage had been sustained when the shaft had stopped so suddenly on impact with the torpedo. He said, 'Go on, Dewhurst.'

'Well, sir, you found the fish was shifting about a little when you went down. Wouldn't it be worth trying to get it on the move properly?'

'How?'

'By giving it a shove off, sir. We can't be much worse off than we are now, nearly in the minefield.'

Cameron glanced across at PO Trent. The torpedo-gunner's mate had pursed his lips and was shaking his head. Cameron asked, 'What do you think, TI?'

'Dunno what to think, sir. What did *you* think, when you was down there?'

'I gave it a bit of a push. It was jammed somewhere below, that was my impression. The back end's free, more or less.'

'So the nose could impact on something.'

'Yes.'

'It's a hell of a risk, sir.'

Dewhurst said loudly, 'It's a hell of a risk already. We're sitting on sudden death as it is. If more aircraft come in, or E boats, we've all had it. And don't forget the minefield.'

Once again, Cameron caught Trent's eye. The TI said, 'There's something in what 'e says, sir.' He sounded doubtful all the same.

Cameron turned away and began pacing the deck, filled with anxiety, knowing that time was desperately short. At any moment the *Burnside*, obviously inside the minefield or very close to it, might hit another mine. As he paced, Dewhurst approached him, blocking his path. Dewhurst said, 'If you'll give the word, sir, I'd like to go down myself.'

'You?' Cameron was rocked.

'Yes, sir. That's why I spoke in the first place. I know I've a reputation for being cack-handed. I know all that. But I'd do my best. I'd like a chance, sir.'

Cameron stared at him. To take the lowest view, Dewhurst was the most easily expendable of any of his small number of seamen; but any slip would send them all to Kingdom Come. On the other hand, to do nothing but wait for the end, the inevitable end, was pretty craven when they just might have a chance . . . it was Trent who swayed the decision finally. Trent coughed and said, 'Two 'ands would be better than one, sir. I'll go down with 'im.' He paused, expectantly. When he spoke again his tone was crisp. 'Permission to proceed, sir, please?'

'Yes,' Cameron said.

*   *   *

Burnside was not informed immediately of what was to be attempted; Cameron preferred this to be his own responsibility; Fanshawe had his own ship to worry about. But as the word spread throughout the tanker, the comments were lurid. Leading Seaman York couldn't believe his ears, was convinced by now that the officer had gone stark, staring mad. So must the TI have done, to think of going over the side with bloody Dewhurst. Dewhurst, York said, would now do for them all. First thing he did would be to lash out at the torpedo with his seaboot. Nevertheless, York could see that it was just about the only thing left to try. Pity it had to be Dewhurst, that was all. Even with the TI there, he'd be bound to make a lash-up of it, that stood to reason. Daft prat.

York was detailed to take charge of the line-tending party; two able seamen would tend each of the lifelines, backed up by two ordinary seamen. In the meantime the Chief Engineer and his junior engineer would ensure that there was enough steam to get way on the ship as soon as it was reported safe to do so. If anything went wrong, they would be the first to go, but only by a split second. All lives were hanging on a thread, and that was nothing new in this situation. There was a feeling throughout the ship that they might just as well get it over one way or the other and be done with it. You could only die once. York said as much to Dewhurst when the latter, secured on the lifeline, was about to go over the side. 'And watch your bloody feet,' he added. 'None of us *want* to die, all right?'

'Shut up, York,' Dewhurst said edgily.

York smouldered. 'Cheek. Soon as you get back, my lad, I'll 'ave you.'

'So you have some confidence after all.'

'Bollocks I have. Anyway ... good luck, mate.' York put out a hand and Dewhurst took it, grinned self-consciously, and said he was ready. York saw the line paid out; alongside Dewhurst, Trent was also lowered. Both men had the powerful tank torches as used by Captain Harcourt on his own mission earlier. The TGM carried a steel lever and a wooden mallet supplied from the boatswain's store, these being secured to his body with lengths of codline. The water was lashing up the stern

203

plating as they went down; the wind howled like a banshee in the tanker's rigging, round the wreckage aft. This apart the ship was as silent as it had been all along, an eerie silence for any ship out in deep water.

Alongside York, Cameron peered down, saw the two heads vanish beneath the surface. That was all he would see now until they came up for air, or to report success or failure. If the worst happened, he wouldn't be seeing anything at all. Just one big flash. He glanced at York's face; York was looking lugubrious rather than anything else, certainly not afraid. York, in fact, was pondering on death and was finding himself treating it with curiosity rather than fear. There was no point in fearing it; it came to everyone in the end, even Churchill one day, and bloody Hitler, and the King and Queen. You couldn't escape it so why worry about it. But it would be *interesting*. The Archbishop of Canterbury, when his turn came, might find he'd been talking bollocks the last half century. York thought of the undesirability of going up to heaven along with Dewhurst; sod that for a lark! Dewhurst would even fumble the keys of the Golden Gate or whatever it was they went through by courtesy of St Peter. Dewhurst would fall arse over tit on God's throne and scatter the archangels like seamen clearing the blocks at Pompey barracks when Both Watches was piped. There were other possible difficulties, not just

Dewhurst: women. There were a number of women wronged in greater or lesser degree by Leading Seaman York in his time on earth. They might be vengeful, report him to the Almighty. Rosie in Devonport, Alice in Londonderry, Maxine some years ago in Sydney, Roxanne in Melbourne, a coloured girl in Cape Town whose name he couldn't remember . . . many others, from Pompey to the Clyde via Liverpool. *Earth has not anything to show more fair than all they bastards . . .* or something like that. That bloke Shakespeare? P'rhaps not.

'Keep your mind on it,' Cameron said sharply.

'Sorry, I'm sure, sir.' York peered professionally at the lifelines leading down. They were slack now; they'd got there. He wished them all the luck in the world.

*   *   *

They could see the torpedo quite clearly; it was still where Cameron had reported it, the propellers thrust up, the nose down. Trent pushed at one of the propellors, gingerly, knowing that if it wasn't for the water the hairs on the back of his neck would rise straight up. There was some give, the torpedo swayed gently. It was swaying already from the action of the water and there was a nasty grating noise coming from below. Trent saw Dewhurst going deeper, pulling his body down the rudder post. Over their heads, the tanker's huge screws loomed, somehow evil and threatening. Trent's lungs were bursting: he was forced to the surface. A couple of seconds later Dewhurst surfaced as well. They hung on the lines, gasping, flinging water from their eyes.

Dewhurst asked, 'What do you think, TI?'

'Give us a chance. See anything deeper down, did you?'

'Yes.' Dewhurst's voice was hoarse. 'The nose is about an inch from the stern plating, slanted inwards. Every now and then ... it almost touches. There's quite a lot of thrust behind it, but something's just stopping it.'

'Jesus Christ send down a dove. You found what's holding it?'

'No. I hadn't the breath to get that far. I'm going down for another look.' Dewhurst shouted up to the deck. At a word from Cameron, York lowered away again.

CHAPTER FOURTEEN

Midshipman Harcourt came aft, his face pale but set hard. He reported to Cameron, formally.

'Orders, sir?'

Cameron looked at him and sensed the facts. He said, 'Nothing you can do just now,

206

Mid. Just stand by on the bridge—you'll be wanted soon, with any luck.' He explained what was being attempted. Then he said, 'I'm sorry.'

'He'd have wanted to die at sea. He loved the sea, you know.'

'I expect he did. The sea gets into a man.'

'In command to the last. Almost, anyway.' Harcourt hesitated. 'He didn't speak at all after I got there. But he'd have wanted to thank you for what you're doing for his ship.'

'It's nothing. We're all just doing what we have to do, that's all.' Cameron put a hand on the midshipman's shoulder, 'Look, Mid. Go and get yourself a shot of whisky. Then go to the bridge and stand by to contact the engine-room—all right?'

'Yes, sir.' Harcourt saluted and turned away, swinging himself up on to the flying bridge. Cameron watched him for a moment, making his way for'ard. It would be something for him, to be on his father's bridge, taking over. But thinking of the body below . . . Cameron gave himself a shake. No time to think about bodies, about death. They had lives to live yet. He looked away across the restless sea, towards the *Burnside*, still afloat with her upper deck virtually awash. She might last into Malta or she might not. If the weather worsened further she wouldn't stand much chance even if the mines allowed. Maybe they weren't yet in the minefield, either the destroyer or the tanker. *Burnside* could have caught a floating mine—must have, otherwise, surely, she would have hit more by now. It was as Cameron was thinking about mines that the seaman posted as lookout on the bridge hailed him.

'Mr Cameron, sir! Mine bearing green four-five, sir!'

'God damn!' Cameron ran for the bridge and climbed fast. He put his glasses on the bearing: there it was right enough, a great horned sphere bobbing about in the waves, free of its sinker. Instant death if one of those horns should touch. Cameron cursed again, feeling dead cold inside. The monstrous object was no more than two cables'-lengths off. The gunner's mate had dragged himself to his feet and was propped against the fore screen of the wheelhouse. Cameron said, 'I can't open fire, GI. The reverberations under water when it went up ... they'd interfere with the TI and Dewhurst.'

'Bugger 'em up good an' proper, sir. I suggest you tell the Captain what you're doing, soon as you can. *They*'ll open fire else.'

'Dead right!' Cameron climbed to monkey's-island and began to operate the mechanical semaphore, clumsily enough: he had only his signalling instruction at *King Alfred* to call upon. Fanshawe acknowledged fast; Cameron passed the information.

The reply was terse: *BF. Good luck all the*

same. Next time ask permission first.

Next time: Cameron gave a sour grin. Fanshawe seemed to have a sense of humour after all. He went down again to the bridge. The midshipman said, 'What about bearing-out spars, sir?'

'Do they have them aboard merchant ships?'

'I don't know. But oars from the boats would be just as good.'

'You're right, Mid. Go below and see to it, will you?'

Harcourt went off, sliding fast down the handrails of the ladders. He collected some hands and made for the lifeboats, already free of their canvas covers as a precaution, however useless. As Cameron went back aft he saw Harcourt going to the for'ard end of the tank deck, through the water surging over the lids. With the low freeboard the mine could, with luck, be borne off with the oars, held at bay till the hull had slid past on the drift. If the mine should make its deadly approach farther for'ard, under the flare of the high bows, then they would have had it. The oars wouldn't reach that far.

Trent and Dewhurst were submerged again. During Cameron's absence they had come up several times. York passed the report.

'They've edged it a little clear o' the rudder post, sir. Still jammed solid, though, they don't know where.' He added, 'TI don't look too good. Face like a codfish, sir.'

'How, like a codfish?' Cameron snapped.

'Pale, sir. Very pale. Feelin' the strain if you asks me. 'E's an RFR man. Not in 'is first flush o' youth.' York drew a hand across his nose, looking sombre. 'Nor me either, come to that.' He wasn't bursting with keenness to go down himself, and he believed that the TI was going to need replacing. In that, York was both right and wrong. Next time Dewhurst surfaced he was alone and looking scared. After getting his breath back he called up to the deck, incoherently. Cameron had him pulled up on the lifeline, and he almost collapsed over the bulwarks. When he could speak the news was grim: PO Trent was trapped. Dewhurst believed he must be dead already. The torpedo had shifted and nipped his arm between itself and the rudder. It was immovable. Dewhurst had done his best but had been forced to the surface for air.

'I'm going down,' Cameron said. 'Are you fit to come down with me? I'll need you—you know the current situation, no one else does.'

'I'm all right, sir,' Dewhurst said. He got up on the bulwarks again. Quickly York secured a spare lifeline around Cameron.

*　　　*　　　*

Feeling a shake throughout his body, Midshipman Harcourt reached out with his oar and made contact with the mine. If that oar slipped and smashed into one of the horns, that would be it. The mine rose and fell with the sea, swooping in towards the ship's side, tight-packed TNT heavily on the move. Four oars lunged at it, bearing it off. A lift of the sea took it clear and Harcourt breathed in relief. But it came back in again, and the tanker didn't seem to be moving, the drift was not carrying her clear.

Harcourt sweated. His arms began to feel the strain. It became agony for them all, but no one was going to give in. They held the mine steady for a moment. Harcourt said, 'Now all together—*shove!*'

They shoved. The mine moved away, hung for a moment on a wave, then slid down the other side. About six feet clear of the hull, it lifted to another wave and once again moved towards the tanker. The oars caught it, like hockey sticks jabbing for some outlandish, lethal ball. Harcourt's oar slid on the wet metal and came into hard contact with one of the horns. All his weight was behind it; the horn broke off. Instinctively all hands ducked beneath the bulwarks, a useless enough barricade. Nothing happened. Harcourt got to his feet, his face bloodless. Even mines, it seemed, could be defective—at least in parts: just because one horn hadn't reacted it didn't have to mean the others wouldn't. Once again the oars went out and bore away at sudden

211

death. The mine rolled away, spinning slowly on the surface, then vanished round the flare of the bows. Harcourt ran up the ladder to the fo'c'sle-head and looked over.

The mine was clear now, crossing ahead of the tanker and drifting harmlessly away off the port bow. Suddenly, the midshipman felt drained of life.

*   *   *

After a series of deep breaths, Cameron had gone under. Pulling himself down by means of the rudder-pintles, he found the torpedo-gunner's mate. It was a horrifying sight. Once, on holiday in the west of Ireland, he had come upon a dog in a clear stream outside the city of Galway, a dog that had looked alive beneath the flowing water but was not. It had a rope around its neck and was tethered to a large chunk of rock in the bed of the stream. The fast flow had given it a vibrancy in death; it was standing in an attitude of tugging at the rope, an attitude in which it had died. All its hairs were streaming with the flow and the eyes were open.

That was how Trent looked. The water pulled at his white uniform, billowed out the back of the shirt, and his eyes stared at the wedged torpedo that was trapping his arm. He was obviously dead; timewise, he had to be. Cameron nevertheless tried to free the arm,

212

assisted by Dewhurst.

No use.

Back to the surface for air, lungs at bursting point. Then down again. The torpedo's tail was still moving a little; there had to be some way of freeing it. The difficulty was that of staying down for long enough to do anything effective. From Dewhurst's earlier report, Cameron knew that the torpedo's nose was close to the stern plating. Making a superhuman effort he pulled himself lower in the water. Before he was forced up again there had been just time to see in the torch beam that the nose was gently moving no more than a half-inch from the hull. The explosion could come at literally any second.

Cameron surfaced with Dewhurst. They took agonizing breaths, clinging to the lifelines, gasping, close to exhaustion. Dewhurst said, 'There's just one thing, sir.'

'Yes?'

'The way it's angled. If the wheel was put over to port, the tail would be thrown more directly up-and-down. Might be, anyway— *could* be. If the rudder's movement freed it, it would go straight down under its own weight, I imagine, wouldn't it?'

'Probably. But then it would steady ... I'm no torpedo expert, but its balancing mechanism would right it automatically.'

'It wouldn't necessarily come up slap under the hull, sir. And if we could get under way

213

fast . . .'

Cameron's mind raced. Something had to be done and it might be better to take a chance now, act positively rather than merely linger on towards oblivion. The rescue tug would take time to reach them, could be sunk with its divers by enemy action in the meantime. And Cameron had no confidence that they themselves could survive another attack.

He said, 'You may be right, Dewhurst.' Then a macabre thought struck him. 'What about the TI? If we turn the wheel, then he—'

'Yes, sir. I know. That's part of it.'

Cameron stared. 'What?'

'The body. The rudder pressure will go through the body, sir. That gives it extra thrust to angle the nose away. A kind of—of packing. And it might prevent a dangerous fracture of the metal, a fracture that might set it off.' Dewhurst added. 'Like you . . . I don't know anything about torpedoes. Only the instruction at *King Alfred*. Rudimentary stuff. Enough to know one end from the other.'

Cameron said, 'It's horrible.'

'Yes, sir. But he's dead, isn't he?'

Cameron thought of the trapped body, remembered Trent in life, Trent the happy optimist, always ready with a laugh, a man of no vice whatsoever, one of the good old backbones of the pre-war Navy. But it was true he was dead. Cameron signalled up to the

214

deck, where Leading Seaman York was looking over. York waved back and both the lifelines were hauled in. As Cameron and Dewhurst clambered over the bulwarks York said, 'Put your foot in it, did you, Dewhurst, me bucko tar?'

Dewhurst didn't answer. Cameron said, 'Can it, York. Speak when you're spoken to.'

With Dewhurst, he went fast along the flying bridge. York stared after him, mouth agape. 'Bleedin' 'ell,' he said. 'What's up with Cameron, then? Seen a ghost, or what?' Then he remembered that Trent was still down there and he had the grace to look ashamed. Maybe his mouth was too big on occasions. He rounded on the ordinary seamen tending the lifelines. 'Don't just 'ang about, do something useful, eh? Coil down them lines, pronto. Don't want the ship lookin' like your grandma's back yard, right?'

* * *

The gunner's mate's face was twisted with pain by now and had gone a nasty shade of grey. When Cameron and Dewhurst entered the wheelhouse he said, 'I heard about the TI, sir. Did you—'

'Too late.'

Garter nodded slowly. 'Thought you would be. Poor old Trenty. And the fish?'

Cameron told him the facts, briefly, and

215

added, 'I'm going to take a chance, GI.'

'Do what, sir?'

'Turn the wheel.'

Garter blew out his cheeks. 'On the TI?' He'd got there and didn't like it. For anyone to be mangled like that ... and Trent was a friend, a messmate. *Had* been. But he knew the officer had no choice, allowing that he'd made his mind up to a course of action.

Cameron explained his intentions and asked, 'Does it make sense, GI? Could it work, d'you think?'

'It's a chance. Evens, I'd say—at best.' Garter gave a ghost of a smile. 'Permission to start praying, sir? Got a lot of leeway to catch up on, I have. Never had the time. Had time to sin, though. Wine, women and song, you know what I mean, all the things the Holy Joes says is wicked.' He was talking to cover up a bad attack of nerves. Enemy attack was one thing, to calmly turn the ship's wheel and die was another. You knew exactly when it would come. You could begin counting the seconds, count your life away to eternity where you mustered by the open list in front of God.

Cameron didn't respond. His face tight, he moved to the engine-room voice-pipe. He blew down. The answer came from the starting platform. Garter heard it: 'Engine-room, Chief Engineer here.'

'Bridge, Chief. I'm going to turn the engines in a few moments. Is everything ready?'

'All ready, yes. What about that torpedo?'

Cameron said steadily, 'It's still there. But I believe it's going to shift harmlessly.'

There was a hard laugh. 'You mean you hope so!'

'That's right, Chief. It's all we can do.'

'Then bloody good luck to us all, laddie.'

'Thank you, Chief.' Cameron replaced the voice-pipe cover. He went into the bridge wing and called to Harcourt, still on mine watch for'ard. 'We're going to move, Mid.'

Harcourt saluted. 'Aye, aye, sir.'

Garter said, 'You going to inform *Burnside*, sir?'

'No. I don't want to waste any more time.' Explanations by signal would take far too long and that torpedo's nose was much too close now. Cameron turned to the man standing by the wheel; he said, 'Take off the lashings.'

Quickly the helmsman cast off the ropes securing the wheel against movement. 'All ready, sir.'

Cameron glanced at the set face of the gunner's mate, who had turned to stare fixedly towards the stern, as though fascinated by the thought of what he might be about to see. Then, taking a deep breath, Cameron passed the orders.

'Wheel hard-a-port. Stand by main engines.'

*   *   *

Fanshawe was sitting on his high chair on his bridge, his mind almost a blank. Thought seemed in a way pointless, a mere exacerbation of the mind. Either he abandoned or he didn't; and so long as the destroyer seemed capable of remaining just about afloat, he reckoned he could do nothing but wait for the rescue tug. There was no real point, he had come to see, in abandoning anyway. Not much use abandoning into a minefield, and the *British Racer* certainly offered no safe refuge for his depleted ship's company. To anchor his mind on something he reflected upon Leading Seaman Dewhurst who would have to be dealt with if ever they reached Malta. No doubt Dewhurst was being a confounded liability aboard the tanker, a bloody nuisance to Cameron. Fanshawe still didn't know what to do about him but was inclining towards disrating the fellow. It wouldn't be fair to lumber someone else with him, not as a leading hand. After disrating he could hardly remain in the ship—that would be unfair too. Perhaps he could be landed to Fort St Angelo, the shore base in Malta, for disposal. He couldn't do much damage in a place where all there was to do between the falling bombs was to sweep the parade ground and then loaf around the Malta bars.

Fanshawe turned and looked aft. Good grief, the ship was a shambles! Water was being shipped from aft almost as far as the fore end of the midship superstructure and the feel of her was horrible, like a suet pudding labouring in marmalade sauce. No life, no vibrancy. The guns' crews still manned their weapons, or such of them as would be able to fire, which in fact wasn't many. The after mountings were submerged, as of course were the after magazines; and the 4-inch HA simply had half the length of its barrel protruding from the surging sea. Fanshawe could only thank God for the relative proximity of the main convoy escorts, some of whom would soon be returning this way to Gibraltar while the others went on through the Med for Alexandria with the rest of the convoy, the part bound for the reinforcement of the Eastern Mediterranean . . .

There was a report, half incredulous, from the leading signalman. 'She's under way, sir!'

Fanshawe swung round. 'What did you say? Who's under way?'

'*British Racer*, sir! She's bloody *moving*, sir!'

Fanshawe snapped, 'God damn it, Cameron's got no right to get under way without permission!' Then he ticked over: the tanker hadn't blown up. He felt sweat pour down his face, felt an uncontrollable shake in his hands. He moved to the gyro repeater and called the wheelhouse.

'Cox'n . . . the tanker's under way. It looks as though the situation's improving.'

It had been the most terrifying moment of Cameron's life. The wheel in the helmsman's grip had seemed stiff, moving against those known obstructions, then it had come free and had gone hard over and there had been a terrible moment of waiting. Cameron had believed he had felt a slight waggle of the stern as of a weight coming off, but this could have been in his imagination: the weight of a torpedo wouldn't be anything like enough ... but the tanker remained intact and the order had gone down for the engines to be put ahead. Slow at first, then faster, and the screw started to bite and water boiled up below the counter and they were on the move. Cameron felt weak at the knees; Garter was grinning and mopping his face.

'Skipper'll be like the bloody cat, sir—having kittens.' He looked at Cameron's taut face. He said, 'It's all right now, sir. Musso permitting, that is. We're away and shipshape. Going to take the old *Burnside* in tow, are you?'

Wordlessly, Cameron nodded. They would have a go at it. He was thinking of PO Trent. He couldn't help it. There would be nothing left. What did one tell the widow? As little as possible was the only answer to that. Just the central truth: that Trent had died a hero. He should get a posthumous decoration. Cameron would see that he did, for what it was worth. He called down to the midshipman.

'Prepare to tow for'ard, Mid. Dewhurst, get below and see that watches are set.' Cameron paused. Then he said, 'Your suggestion paid off. I'm very grateful ... not to say *bloody* grateful. Well done.'

Dewhurst flushed, saluted and turned away. Outside in the bridge wing he met Leading Seaman York. York said, 'I 'appened to over'ear the eulogy. I dunno! With some blokes cack-'andedness moves so bleedin' fast it catches up with its own arse in a manner o' speakin'. Things comes right by accident.' He sniffed. 'What I mean is, I second the officer's remarks. Well done. Mrs York'll be delighted.'

Dewhurst grinned. 'Somehow I doubt it, Stripey!'

'Stripey my arse, I'm a leadin' 'and. Don't be bloody impertinent.' York took a mock swipe at him. 'Piss off.'

'Piss off yourself,' Dewhurst said, and went down the ladder. York stared after him, scratching his head, steel helmet tilted flat aback. Bloody Dewhurst, he'd got bloody cocky all of a sudden, didn't become him. Never mind the weird movements of his brain, if any, he was still the most cack-handed seaman York had ever come across.

*   *   *

221

Later that day, as dusk began to come down, the rescue tug made contact. Fanshawe signalled her: *Do not require your immediate assistance but would like you to stand by.* He owed Cameron that. Cameron would have the satisfaction, if all continued to go well, of completing the tow into the Grand Harbour, now a matter of fifteen hours' steaming ahead at their slow speed. The weather had moderated a little and during the afternoon some blue sky had broken through the overcast. A destroyer and a corvette had come out from Malta with the rescue tug, and more Seafires plus Beaufighters roared over their heads. The cruisers and aircraft carriers from the outward convoy were steaming towards them, bound for Gibraltar. Musso wouldn't stick his neck out any more now. Fanshawe paced his small bridge in a much happier frame of mind. A number of signals had been exchanged with the tanker and there had been a shouted conversation while Cameron had closed *Burnside* preparatory to passing the tow. Even the matter of Dewhurst seemed settled: one couldn't bring a charge against him now, at any rate not a serious one. Just something to satisfy King's Regulations, a charge of carelessness perhaps. There was a sense of euphoria around and the suddenly raised spirits were sublimating it in what Fanshawe considered a ridiculous display of sentiment about the ship's cat. Even the

222

coxswain, sober old CPO Dickens, hadn't proved immune. He'd made a solemn request for Beano to be rated leading cat—just as though the animal had been responsible for their deliverance. The excuse had been that she'd given birth in time to bring them all good luck, as if she'd had any choice in the matter. For a cat on Clydeside the problem was how to avoid a pregnancy, not how to acquire one.

Early next morning the breakwater was in sight beneath a sky now clear of all cloud. A brilliant day, with Malta lying sand-coloured and battle-scarred in the sunshine. As the ships passed slowly through into the Grand Harbour a storm of cheering came from Fort St Angelo, from Custom House Steps, from Lascaris, from all the warships lying alongside or at the buoys. Congratulatory signals came from Vice-Admiral, Malta, and from His Excellency the Governor. It was a great occasion: the *British Racer* with her full cargo to keep the defence in being was a welcome sight. But as the harbour tugs came out to take over the remnant of the destroyer, and the tow was cast off, Fanshawe on his bridge and Cameron aboard the tanker were thinking not about the celebratory noises but of the price paid. There were many letters that would have to be written now to the families at home—the families of both crews. By this time the after pump-room had been reached and opened up. The boatswain, Gutteridge, was still in there, blackened and unrecognizable, roasted. He was just one.

The gunner's mate, propped against the woodwork of the tanker's bridge wing, summed it all up with a quotation. He said, ' "If blood be the price of Admiralty," sir . . . I reckon you know the rest.'

Cameron nodded. Lord God, they *had* paid in full! He made an attempt to lighten the atmosphere. He said, 'Well, GI, I suppose you'll be down the Gut tonight.'

'Me, sir?' Garter's eyebrows rose. 'With this back? I'd be about as much bloody use as a flea at a bullfight. One heave and I'd lock solid.'

Through the cheering and the waved caps of the fleet they moved on for the buoy.

We hope you have enjoyed this Large Print book. Other Chivers Press or Thorndike Press Large Print books are available at your library or directly from the publishers.

For more information about current and forthcoming titles, please call or write, without obligation, to:

Chivers Press Limited
Windsor Bridge Road
Bath BA2 3AX
England
Tel. (01225) 335336

OR

Thorndike Press
P.O. Box 159
Thorndike, Maine 04986
USA
Tel. (800) 223-2336

All our Large Print titles are designed for easy reading, and all our books are made to last.